Also by Nuala Ní Chonchúir

Novel

You (New Island, 2010)

Short Fiction

Nude (Salt, 2009)
To the World of Men, Welcome (Arlen House, 2005 & 2011)
The Wind Across the Grass (Arlen House, 2004 & 2009)

Poetry

The Juno Charm (Salmon Poetry, 2011)
Portrait of the Artist with a Red Car (Templar Poetry, 2009)
Tattoo: Tatú (Arlen House, 2007)
Molly's Daughter (Arlen House, 2003; in *Divas! New Irish Women's Writing Anthology*)

MOTHER AMERICA

About the Author

Nuala Ní Chonchúir is a short story writer, novelist and poet. Born in Dublin in 1970, she lives in Galway with her husband and three children.

Nuala has won many short fiction awards, including RTÉ Radio's Francis MacManus Award, the *Dublin Review of Books* Flash Fiction Prize, the Cúirt New Writing Prize, the inaugural Jonathan Swift Award and the Cecil Day Lewis Award. She was shortlisted for the European Prize for Literature.

Mother America is her fourth short story collection. Her story 'Peach', from the collection, has been nominated for a 2012 Pushcart Prize.

www.nualanichonchuir.com

MOTHER AMERICA

and other stories

Nuala Ní Chonchúir

NEW ISLAND

Mother America
First published 2012 by
New Island
2 Brookside
Dundrum Road
Dublin 14

www.newisland.ie

P/B	ISBN	978-1- 84840-159-4
ePub	ISBN	978-1- 84840-160-0
mobi	ISBN	978-1- 84840-161-7

British Library Cataloguing Data. A CIP catalogue record for this
book is available from the British Library.

Cover design by Inka Hagen
Typeset by JM Infotech INDIA
Printed by ScandBook AB, Sweden

New Island received financial assistance from
The Arts Council (An Comhairle Ealaíon), Dublin, Ireland

For my mother, Nuala,
and the ones I mother – Cúán, Finn and Juno

Acknowledgements

Thanks goes to the editors of the following publications where many of these stories were published: *Accenti; Crannóg; Dublin Review of Books; Faceless Monsters* anthology; *The Irish Times; Necessary Fiction; Prairie Schooner; Ropes 2012; Shine On: Irish Writers for Shine* anthology (Dedalus Press); *Sparks 12; Take a Leap e-anthology* (Cloudscapes); *What the Dickens?; Willesden Herald: New Short Stories 4* anthology (Pretend Genius Press).

'The Egg Pyramid' won the *Dublin Review of Books* Flash Fiction Prize; 'Moon Hill' was placed second in the Accenti Writing Contest (Canada); 'When the Hearse Goes By' was runner-up in the Short Fiction Prize (UK); 'Peach' won the Jane Geske Award and was nominated for a Pushcart Prize (USA).

Thanks to the Tyrone Guthrie Centre at Annaghmakerrig where some of these stories were written. Special thanks to Deirdre O'Neill and Eoin Purcell. And *míle buíochas* to all those from whom I borrowed and begged stories and words.

Contents

Peach

There was a pregnant woman getting drunk in the back lounge; I could see her through the hatch, from where I sat at the bar. She was drinking and crying, sitting on the red velveteen couch alone. Chuffy wiped glasses, poured another Cidona for me, and served the few other customers. He looked over at the woman then nodded in my direction, as a way of asking if I had seen her. I shrugged, to indicate that I had, and watched her. She looked healthy and out of place. We never got many women in The Cova, especially ones we didn't know. Most of us were regulars, bent out of shape by loneliness; we welcomed any intrusion.

The woman sobbed loudly and wrapped her hands around her belly, as if it were a beach ball she was about to throw. Her head drooped forward and I could see tears splashing down her shirt. I wondered what was wrong with her. Maybe, I thought, the baby's father had walked out. Maybe, like most of us, the rough magic of her childhood haunted her and she hoped for a better life for her kid. Or, maybe, she didn't want the child at all.

Chuffy walked over and dropped a box of tissues onto her table; she looked up, startled. He put his hand on her shoulder.

'You should think about calling it a night,' he said.

'There's no point.'

'Drinking for two is not really the thing. You know that.'

The woman grimaced. 'It's too late,' she said, 'he's already gone.'

I was at the Corporation Market, buying fish for my Friday-night kedgeree, when I saw Chuffy trundling down one of the cluttered aisles opposite me. I slotted my fingers inside my lips to whistle but, at that moment, he turned and spoke to a woman walking beside him. Looking at her long hair and the curved egg of her stomach, I realised it was the crying woman from the bar. I pulled my fingers from my mouth and stared. Chuffy's head dipped close to hers, to hear whatever it was she had said in reply to him. They looked intimate and familiar and I was surprised to find that I felt put out.

I watched Chuffy in The Cova that evening, wondering whether to ask about the woman. Chuffy was fatherly, avuncular even, and he was growing old in that Irish way: the nose and chin sloping towards each other; the skewed, dark pools of his eyes getting lost in his face. I wanted to quiz him about how well he knew the woman – if he really knew her – but my curiosity baffled me, so I didn't ask.

'It's dead tonight,' I said, looking around at the mostly empty tables.

'I might close soon and be damned,' Chuffy said, flicking the remote at the television and talking over his shoulder to me.

'Were you here earlier?' I said.

'I came in at six. Waste of bloody time.'

'I got a nice bit of smoked haddock at Stony's stall today,' I said.

'He had nothing left by the time I got there; another bloody waste of time. Drink that back there, Dominic; I'm going to close her up,' Chuffy said, flicking the lights behind the bar to let people know he was shutting for the evening.

*

There was a commotion going on around the phone box at the end of my road; I strolled past and surveyed the huddle of heads in the group that had gathered. One or two people were looking up and down the street, as if searching for answers or an escape. There was someone lying on the ground, half-in and half-out of the phone box; the receiver was dangling. It was the woman from the pub.

'Maud,' a man said. 'Maud! Can you hear me?'

I knelt down. 'She's pregnant,' I said.

'Not anymore she's not,' the man said and stood up.

'You know her?'

'Not really; she used to work in Creaven's shop. Her name is Maud. Maud Peach.' The man shrugged and walked away.

Maud opened her eyes and looked at me; I checked her over and put my hand under her head. She wasn't cut or bleeding that I could see.

'You'll be OK,' I said, 'no damage done. Better before you're twice married and once a widow.' She smiled and I helped her to sit. 'I'm a friend of Chuffy's from The Cova; I'm Dominic. Can you get up, Maud?'

'My arm hurts. I think I fainted.' She hung her head and moaned; I helped her to her feet and brought her to rest on a low garden wall. Her jewellery was optimistic, I noticed, almost childish: an orange plastic bangle and a strand of multicoloured wooden beads.

'I'll ring for an ambulance,' I said.

'Don't. Just take me home.'

At Maud's front door a smoke-coloured cat with white feet brushed around my legs and pushed its torso into my shins. I half-kicked it away, being careful not to hurt it.

'Your cat?' I asked, while Maud unlocked the door.

'No, that's Chicago; he belongs to the neighbour.' She shook her foot at him. 'Psst, Chicago, psst. Get lost.' Chicago ran through Maud's legs into the hall; he looked up at us. 'I should stop feeding him,' she said.

*

There was a tension to the way Maud occupied her rooms. Even though she had invited me to come to her house, I could tell that her routine was upset in a way that she did not altogether welcome. She was straining to be hospitable and I felt as if she expected me to entertain her but didn't trust me to succeed; it made me uncomfortable. I hadn't seen her since I had left her to the door the day she fell.

'How are you since?' I said.

'Grand now; not a bother.'

'Will I open the wine?' I said, pointing at the bottle I had brought.

'Sure. I'll get a couple of glasses.'

'None for me; I'll have water.'

'Oh?' she said.

'Drinking gets in the way of my suffering.'

I laughed to kill the sorry weight of the comment. Maud smiled but looked unsure. She uncorked the wine, held it up to her nose and sniffed deep into the neck of the bottle.

'It covers mine,' she said.

There was a Kahlo-bright oilcloth on her table: it was yellow with cerise hibiscus flowers. An orchid, propped in a milk bottle, spilled orange dust from its stamen onto the tablecloth; the orchid seemed to spray its hot smell into the room. A birdcage on a stand was parked in one corner. I looked in at a budgie; he was a startling, fake-looking blue.

'Wow, he's attractive.'

'This is Droopy,' Maud said. 'He's such a little pet.' She laughed and flicked her fingers at the bird. 'Hello beautiful Droopy. Hello boy!' She peeped and trilled at him before putting on a CD and sitting opposite me at the table, her back straight; the wheen of an overblown love song filled the room.

Maud was beautifully old-fashioned, I thought, with her long hair and simple t-shirt – like something from a 1970s film. Her lips were aristocratically full and she had the kind of tail-ended hair that I always wanted to gather in handfuls and press to my face.

I guessed, by the tense way she held herself, that she spent a lot of time on her own. I wanted to ask about her baby but couldn't seem to get the words to form right; I thought that it must have died and I didn't want to be nosey or insensitive. She looked different on the other side of the pregnancy: her cheeks were less fleshy, she was milk-pale, and lethargy oozed off her despite her nervousness. I had an urge to make things better for her, to help in some way by saying something that would heal her a little. But she was one of those chatless people, the kind that doesn't feel the need to talk unless you make the conversation happen for them. And anyway, I didn't have a clue what I should say.

'Ah, I'll have a glass of wine,' I said, suddenly feeling the need for that prop.

'Lovely.'

Maud looked brighter as she got up to get me a glass. The wine had a soapy aftertaste but I liked it. We didn't talk much, but sat listening to the music. When we had finished the bottle of wine, I felt like a previous version of myself; someone more interested in things, more able. It was a short-lived high. I heard a train chuntering past on the tracks nearby and its long, lonely whistle cut through the spell, making me myself again. I looked out at the crimson tops of the maple trees in Maud's garden, then at the wine glass in my hand, and wondered again about her child.

'No more wine for me or I'll be twisted,' I said, putting down the glass.

'Come on, Dominic; I'm fed up drinking on my own.' She wiggled my hand. 'Just a little more. A "dropeen", as my mother used to say.'

'I will so,' I said, 'I'll have a dropeen.'

Maud smiled; the first genuine smile I'd ever seen on her mouth. I wanted to kiss her then and my euphoria for the promise of the evening returned. She filled fresh glasses with Prosecco produced from the fridge and pointed to the sofa where we then sat. I watched the bubbles squirting upwards in my glass, as seductive as a light show; I took Maud's hand.

'Tell me about your baby,' I said, in the gentlest voice I could muster.

'Oh God,' she said, and I put my arm around her. She took a tube of rose salve from her pocket, buttered it onto one finger and slicked her lips with it. She tried to talk but began to sob and I held her and let her cry until she seemed ready. Instead of speaking she got up and lifted a photo-frame from the mantle-piece. She handed it to me – a photo of a newborn. Her baby, I presumed. It looked ugly in the way all babies look ugly to me. I nodded to indicate approval of some sort, sure she could read my disinterest in the child, or at least in how it looked.

'Sweet,' I said, eventually.

'So beautiful,' Maud said, taking the photo from me. She started to cry again. 'Look at his head: wrinkled velvet. I've never touched anything as pure.' She bent forward and hiccupped, dragging grief down into her throat.

'A boy,' I said. 'What did you call him?'

'I had no say in naming him. He's not my son; he belongs to my sister and her husband. They called him Max.'

She bent forward and cried into her hands, her hair over her face. Her body jiddered and shook; I kept my arms around her and she cried and cried. Her tears were huge and snot streeled from her nose; I handed her some tissues. Her weeping reminded me of the lavishly grieving mothers of TV news – Muslim women shaking their hands, groaning into aprons, the dead child swaddled in some horribly ordinary floral cloth. Years of love reduced to public wailing and a small body rocked above a crowd, passing roughly from hand to hand. At least they had a process, I thought; Maud, it seemed, was left with nothing.

'It's hard going,' I said, 'to carry a baby for so long and then…'

8

'The worst of it is, that's not even the worst of it. They led me to believe I'd have a relationship with him, you know? A really close auntie-nephew relationship. But they've left. They're gone to live three thousand miles away, to Boston, and I'll hardly ever see them. See him. They had it planned; they must have had it planned for ages.'

'Christ.' I didn't know what to say; I patted her hair.

'I feel like my whole head – my body – is in some sort of dystopia these last few months; I'm me but I'm not me. Do you know what I mean?'

'You're grieving,' I said. 'It's normal. I was like that after I separated from my wife; life was blurry for about two years.'

'I wouldn't have thought you could grieve for the living.'

'Of course you can.'

'It's all Roger's fault – my brother-in-law; my sister wouldn't have had the wit to come up with it.' She explained that the surrogacy had been Roger's idea in the first place and he controlled his wife's life in a way that frightened Maud. 'Now look what he's done, the prick; he's taken them both away from me.' She swigged her wine. 'He's one of those conservative, determined types. You know, plays golf every Sunday; wears navy shirts with white cuffs and collars. How could anyone trust a man who dresses like that?'

I laughed loudly. It was one of those outbursts that sounds as insane and pointless as canned laughter on TV. I was trying to force lightness into the mood, into the room, but it came out wrong. Maud stared at me. I didn't speak but breathed deeply on the smell in the air that was like the smell in a seldom-used church. Suddenly all I could think of was escape; her drama was too much for me. She took my hand and kissed my knuckles; I looked at her sad face and relaxed a little.

Later, in bed, I lay over her and pinched her ear lobes gently. I'd watched her slip out the silver stems of her earrings as she stood naked before her dressing table and I wanted to feel the piercings in her ears for myself. I pressed my forefinger and thumb over the knots the holes made in her lobes and whispered, 'Maud.' I kissed her mouth. She was already sliding into sleep and didn't kiss back. I slumped onto one elbow. 'Maud, are you awake?'

'No.' She didn't open her eyes.

I woke feeling as if I had two ribcages and one was pressing on the other; I thought my chest was going to break. It was a long time since I'd had a hangover. My brain was dull as a boiled egg but a pink-green aurora borealis insisted on dancing behind my closed eyes, making me feel like I was swirling in space. The pillow smelled – beautifully – of Maud's hair, and that smell was like limes: tangy and bitter-citrusy. It intoxicated me even in my hungover state. She wasn't in the bed or even in the room.

I got up and stood at the window that overlooked the train tracks. A breeze block wall was covered in graffiti: 'Mooney is an ape'. 'Sam and Jen are smelly fools'. 'Dicey R.I.P.'.' There were other artistic squiggles of words that I couldn't decipher. The tracks were littered with screeds of used toilet roll; plastic bags jigged in the trees.

Maud's house had a stillness that I found almost unbearable, a sense of time being immoveable; I needed noise. I stood and looked out the window and wanted to run. I pulled on my clothes, determined to leave as soon as I could.

*

When my wife and myself split up, I felt as if I had been turned inside out. The day I left her, my body and head hummed in a delirious trance. I knew I was doing the right thing but, at the same time, I didn't know anything. There was somewhere to go – I had already rented a flat – but that wasn't where I wanted to be. Even though I had no real history with the coastline, all I wanted that day was to stand beside the sea and look at it. The sea was, I suppose, associated in my mind with hazy childhood trips to Brittas Bay and Portrane. Maybe I was trying to grab at the comfort blanket of being a small child on an excursion. Were they really happy, those jaunts, I wonder now? Did my parents manage not to poke at each other's soft underbellies for even a few hours, so we could enjoy ourselves?

It didn't matter that day; my marriage was over, and, like an invalid, I craved the freshness of the sea wind, the briny smell, the danger and beauty of a wide expanse of water. Though I was never much of a swimmer or fisherman, something about the sea's power drew me out to Dublin Bay and I sat on a bench for hours drinking in the air, staring at the bouncing grey waters.

Now I wanted to do something helpful for Maud and it was the sea that occurred to me again. It had soothed me that morning and I thought it might help Maud too.

We walked arm-in-arm down O'Connell Street and I felt absurdly whole with Maud beside me. We passed the woman who preached in silence on the central aisle, waving her rosary beads and pacing; her elegant black dress complimenting the hair that sat in a grey cob on her head.

'God love her,' Maud muttered.

I didn't feel sorry for the woman – she seemed happy always – but I wasn't inclined to disagree with Maud. We trotted down Talbot Street to the train station, me feeling as if I owned the town with her on my arm.

A pair of hawk-nosed girls with red hair sat opposite us on the train. I smiled at them but they stared out of flat eyes and didn't smile back. Kids have always scared me; weird ones make me feel dunderingly inadequate, so I sat in silence, looking across Maud to the passing views of people's bedrooms, back-gardens and washing lines and, eventually, the sea.

When Ireland's Eye hoved into view, Maud flickered with excitement. 'Look, Dominic,' she said, grabbing my hand, 'the Eye. We can take a boat over to there you know. Chuffy brought us once.'

'Did he?' I said, surprised by this snippet as much as by her mention of him. My throat dried up and I could feel the tinny thump of my heart. 'How do you know Chuffy?' I asked at last.

'Chuffy is Roger's uncle,' she said. 'He knows all about Max, about what happened.'

'God, he never mentioned a thing,' I said, realising that Chuffy didn't talk about anything much beyond the TV news, or bits and pieces from the lives of The Cova's few regulars.

'Chuffy's good to me, he listens.'

'He's a listener all right,' I said.

We decided to walk down Harbour Road – Maud wanted to look at the big houses. She called out their names as we passed them: 'Inishowen, Lynwood, Errigal, Kincora.' Their gardens were enormous and rich with rowan, willow and oak trees. We came to a shop which was also a pub.

'Beer, books, eggs, marble, wool, souvenirs, ice creams,' Maud read from a sign on the front.

A plastic Angelito cone – the size of a man – was fixed to the top of a gas cylinder outside. I went in and got us a 99 each. Maud smiled like a child when I handed her the cone and I watched with pleasure as her tongue flicked over the ice cream. We crossed the road and sat on a rough stone wall overlooking the sea, near to an old couple who were also eating cones. The way they were dressed – both in beige, the woman in man's shoes – and the sloppy, intent way they ate their ice creams made me feel sad; I finished my own one quickly, keeping my eyes focused on the harbour.

Children were throwing fish heads to three fat seals further along and the wind thwacked the mast ropes of the boats that were moored below us. The seals smiled and ducked, ate and bobbed; the children laughed. My skin felt salt-blown and tight, a feeling I loved. The sea's smell and Maud's shoulder under my arm made me feel secure. I hugged her side to my side and she grinned at me. We walked then, past the bandstand and down to the yacht club, looking at all the parents entertaining babies on the grass and the busy boat-owners who fit so naturally into the place. We scouted a few restaurant menus but Maud said she would prefer to make dinner for us.

We walked to her house from the train station. Chicago was sitting on the doorstep, licking himself, and he ran inside as soon as the door was open. I like cats about as much as I like kids, so after a while I tried to toe him out of the room; he wouldn't move. I snarled at him and he turned his back to me and stretched out on the mat as if to stick himself to it.

'Kssss,' I said, flapping my hand at him.

Maud was chopping vegetables at the table. 'Leave him, Dominic,' she said; 'he's doing no harm.'

I sat, sipped wine and tried to adjust myself to the odd atmosphere in the house. The cat lay like a dead thing and Maud cooked quietly. Even the budgie was silent.

After dinner we sat on the sofa and kissed. The wine made my tongue fuller, her lips softer, and we kissed for a long time like teenagers afraid to do more.

'The sea was nice,' I said, turning her hair on my fingers.

'It did me good.' She kissed my nose, my eyes, my mouth.

'Do you want to go to the bedroom?' I asked.

'Let's do it here,' Maud said.

I tucked her under me and slowly removed her skirt and underwear. We made love with the sour smell of the cushions in our noses.

Like a slow walker on ice, I am always waiting for the worst to happen. Or if not the worst, then something untoward. My wife, sick of my downbeat attitudes, once said to me: 'People don't live in single states of mind, Dominic. You can't let yourself live in a single state of mind.' But I always have – dread is my default position – and I was surprised to realise that everybody else isn't the same. So, though I was enjoying getting to know Maud, I was always waiting for something to crop up.

We fell asleep on the sofa. Maud woke me in the night and we fumbled, naked, to her bedroom and snuggled down together under the quilt. I realised I needed the loo and got up again. I don't like sleeping nude, so on my way back from the toilet I dipped into the sitting-room to retrieve my boxers and t-shirt. I could hear little fossicking noises and I followed them to the corner and Droopy's birdcage. He was scrabbling around the bottom of the cage, burbling, his head hanging down; I thought he looked unwell. I opened the door and poked gently at him with my finger. He lifted his face to me and cocked his head; I was amazed when he jumped onto my finger. I slowly lifted out my hand through the birdcage door and looked closely at him. He puffed his tiny blue chest and raised his wings.

'I think you're OK,' I said, and went to put him back on his perch, but he flew off around the room. 'Fuck,' I said, and lunged towards him but I couldn't catch him. I jumped after him again and knocked over a chair. He settled on the curtain rail. 'Come here, Droopy,' I called and stood with my arm out; I thought I might coax him down somehow if I stayed still. He took off again, flying into the middle of the room. As if in slow motion I saw Chicago arc through the air and settle his jaws around Droopy's upper body. He shook the bird hard; I leapt forward and belted the cat with my hand.

'You fucker,' I shouted; 'let go, let go.'

Maud appeared in the doorway. 'Oh,' she said, 'oh.'

Chicago dropped Droopy and skulked under the sofa. I bent and picked up the budgie; he felt soft, insubstantial. His neck wobbled and his head flopped comically from side to side. I waggled him a bit.

'He's really droopy now,' I said, and held him up for Maud to see. I laughed.

Maud burst out crying.

*

I got footless. I decided I would take the train out to Howth and sit on the wall by the sea in the dark, but the last train was already gone when I arrived at the station. Carrying a bottle of cider under my jacket and taking what must have been obvious swigs – though I was attempting to be furtive – I launched down the quays, heading who-knows-where.

Rory O'More Bridge was lit up, bright blue and inviting, as I came near to it. I stood on Usher's Island, staring at the bridge reflected in the black Liffey and at Wolfe Tone Quay opposite; I looked at the steps that seemed to prance down into the water from the quay. I made my way across the bridge and to the river steps; under the street lamp, their mica-glint was like a siren call. Leaving my shoes, jacket and bottle of cider on the footpath, I hopped the wall and ran down the steps, straight into the cold, cold water.

I swam – badly – the width of the Liffey and as I swam I talked to Maud.

'I'm sorry,' I said, 'about the cat. About the budgie. I'm sorry, Maud.' I was crying and shivering, pulling my arms through a clumsy front crawl. 'I'm sorry, Maud,' I sang out, and wondered why the freezing river was not sobering me up. The water stank of mud and it pulled at my body like river weed; I pushed on. 'I'm sorry about your baby, Maud. So sorry about your baby.' I kept up the apologies to Maud like a mantra to get me across the river. 'Forgive me, Maud. I'll make it right. I'm sorry. We'll get a new budgie. Sorry. Sorry.'

I should have drowned; I'm no swimmer. I hauled myself up on to the steps on the opposite quay. I sat, shivering and crying for a while, then I slopped in my wet socks over the bridge to retrieve my things. I tipped the rest of the cider into the Liffey for the fish.

That swim was one of the stupidest things I have ever done, but I'm more ashamed of what I did next. I went to The Cova and threw a rock through the front window. I watched as the glass jagged and shattered; I felt wholly empty. I went home and slept it off.

*

'Dominic,' Chuffy said, as I took my place at the bar. 'Long time,' he said, and poured a Cidona which he set in front of me. If he knew it was me who had broken the window, he didn't say. I thought he must know and I was sick inside.

'Maud?' I said.

'Went to Boston last month,' Chuffy replied.

I sipped my Cidona and looked around to see who else was in.

The Egg Pyramid

There are things you can do when your husband sleeps with your sister. You can sit in your studio and imagine them together, the toad and the mouse. Him moving over her. Her on top of him. You can hear dark skin slap against honey skin; you can hear moans. But he is your toad and she is your mouse – your Diego and your Cristina – so you drown those thoughts because they bring more tears than a blood-letting.

But there are things you can do. You can take the pins from your hair and unweave the plaits. Then you can use a scissors to hack off the lengths. You can scatter the strands on the floor and on your yellow chair, where they lie like snakes. The dogs and monkeys – who still love you – can watch. You can forgo silver rings and turquoise beads. You can dress like a man, in a baggy grey suit and maroon shirt. You can hang your Tijuana dresses in the closet and shut the door on their gaiety.

What else can you do? Well, you can imagine his seed nestling in your sister's womb and blossoming. You can witness a baby – a boy, let's say – making a hard melon of her belly. You have never had a ripe stomach. Three times that might have happened for you; three times you bled your baby out before anyone knew that you too could give life. You can look at your sister's children and ask yourself if they have features that belong to your husband – drooping eyes, full lips, cruelty.

You can count up the seven years you have lived together and you can see that there are plenty of itches to be scratched on both sides. You know that Diego's urge to scratch burns more than yours; his need is eternal. You can leave your house and take a flat in the heart of Mexico, to create a space for your husband to sulk into and for your sister to wonder in. You can fly to New York then hurry home again, because Diego pulls on you the way mother moon pulls on the sea.

Your husband is an accident that happened to you but he is also your north and south. And, because you love him more than your own skin, you can try to accept and you can try to forgive. You can shrug off the pain that pinches like a body brace and throw laughter bombs out into the world to blow up the hurt that remains.

But, when your sister sleeps with your husband, it is like balancing a pyramid of eggs on a glass platter on the top of your head. You dare not move much for fear of what might happen. The best thing that you can do is to take your brush in one hand, your palette in the other, and sit at your easel and paint. Yes, you can paint.

Letters

attie's letter arrived on Tuesday morning and
I saved it, like always, for the evening. For
after my walk on Avenue of the Americas, which I
take to feel like I am alive. For after a coffee with Vito
in the Washington Square Diner, where we indulged
in our small ritual of winks, smiles and chat. For after
a meal of tortellini and a glass of milk, alone in my
apartment; I had no vegetables – the asparagus and
broccoli looked groggy in the heat, so I left them
at the store. These days I say store instead of shop;
messages are now groceries; I say sidewalk not footpath. I will never blend in but with words, I make
some effort.

Mattie was always my favourite, though they say
a mother doesn't have such a thing. He was my best
boy before we left the old country, right up until we
came to New York. His brothers were tougher, gone

from me sooner; Mattie had stuck around my ankles since he was a baby. I named him for his father and, though I don't like to think of that old fool, I always enjoy remembering Mattie as a boy, before he made us come away, leaving all behind.

*

Steam swelled from Mattie's woollen socks.

'Would you ever keep your feet back from the fire, son?' I said.

Mattie grunted, resenting the interruption. He was reading to me from the *Evening Press*, an after-school habit he took on when his father died. I sometimes listened, sometimes didn't; all the stories were sad.

'What?' he said.

'Will you go to the pit? I want to start the dinner,' I said.

He sighed, hunched his body further into the chair, and rattled the newspaper. 'Do you not want to hear the last bit of this?'

'Go on and get me the spuds,' I said, knowing he wouldn't.

I heaved myself up, got the bucket from the pantry, and lifted the back-door latch. The potato pit was covered with flour sacks; I flicked one off and leaned forward, ready to fill the bucket. I stopped. There was a frog on the pile, squatting fat and perfect like a little king; I let a roar and jumped away from the pit. Mattie came running.

'Ma?'

'Jesus, Mary and Joseph. Get it!' I shouted.

'What? What is it?'

'There's a frog. Bring something to trap it in.'

He ran back into the kitchen and fumbled in the dresser. I could hear him banging the drawers and cursing while I stood, trying to keep the frog fixed to its spot by staring at it. The frog's body pulsed and made me feel sick; I willed it not to move. Mattie came out and walked slowly to the pit, his face worried.

'It looks wicked,' he said. The frog lunged forward, a jump that didn't move it far, and I imagined I heard the squelch of its insides; Mattie leapt. 'Jesus, it looks wicked. Wicked!'

'How are you going to catch it?' I said. He held up a sugar bag and a spoon. 'God almighty,' I said, thinking I'd have to throw away the spoon after. A waste.

Mattie knelt by the pit, holding the bag and the spoon. He worried his bottom lip with his teeth. I looked again at the frog; its skin was like an autumn leaf, mottled and dry.

'He's not slimy at all,' I said.

'It's awful big. For a frog.'

'Go on, son, get him.'

The frog looked ahead lazily, its cheeks twitching. Then it belched and jumped again; its skin changed from brown to green in the evening light.

'The fecker,' Mattie shrieked, and fell onto his behind.

'Catch it, Mattie. Spoon it in, come on. Oh God.' I felt giddy and wanted to laugh, though I was afraid;

I pulled my skirt closer to my legs, thinking of the frog's skin touching my own.

'I'm telling you, it looks wicked,' Mattie said.

His brothers came back in the middle of it all; Stephen stood in the doorway.

'What's going on, Ma?'

'Look, there's a huge frog on the potato pit. He's lepping about.'

Stephen laughed. He lunged forward, grabbed the frog into his big hands, and hooshed it over the back wall. Johnny crowded behind Stephen, laughing at Mattie, who was still holding the sugar bag and spoon. I clipped Johnny on the ear to shut him up, but he laughed more.

Stephen and Johnny called Mattie 'Wicked' for a while after that; I said not to mind them.

*

Now there's no back yard, no fireplace, no potato pit. There are seven storeys below me and three above; I never imagined people lived in any way but our own, until Mattie brought me here. He brought me here and left me here, to go as far away again to the other coast, to a place full of Mexicans.

My view is of glass-fronted blocks and an old brownstone that huddles between two taller buildings; I have to lean out to see the street below, but its noises come clearly to me: sirens, banging trash-cans, shouting, and endless cars with tooting horns. This city is always on the go.

I walk on Tuesday along Avenue of the Americas. Mattie's letter is a comforting, papery wad in my pocket. I haven't carried a handbag since a dirty-faced girl dragged me to the ground trying to pull it from my hands. My legs got scraped but the little bitch didn't get my bag; she hadn't reckoned on the strength of an Irish mother. These days I carry all my bits and bobs – money, hankie, keys – in my pockets, like a man.

The Avenue is throbbing as it always is with hucksters and mad-men and ordinary people doing ordinary things: shopping, arguing, hurrying. I've never known such a place for haste. I'm glad to leave the busy Avenue for The Washington Square Diner. My back is clammy with sweat when I push open the door; it's cool inside. Vito is sitting at the window, his behind lapping over the sides of a high stool like rising dough.

'Bridie,' he says, getting down off the stool; 'when will you be my bride?' He kisses my hand and leads me into my booth.

'Vito, like I tell you every week, I've been up the aisle once already and that was enough for me.' I smile.

'You break my heart,' he says, and claps his meaty hands across his chest. He brings us two coffees and winks. I wink back. Vito is fat – fatter than me – and he already has a wife. 'And how is your son, Bridie?' he says.

'I have his letter right here.' I pull it from my pocket. Vito takes the letter and fingers it; he stares at the sealed envelope, the stamp, my address and Mattie's, as if it all might tell him something.

'So many words, so many letters,' he says, and hands it back to me.

'Yes, Vito, there are so many words. So many letters.'

We sip our coffee and Vito squeezes my fingers in his plump ones. 'I love you, Bridie. Really,' he says.

'You're a silly old man, Vito.'

The heat swaddles me when I leave the diner, wrapping itself around my face and body; it pulls the breath from my lungs and makes me gasp. The whole city is muffled under this blanket of still air. The coffee has made me hotter than before and the grocery store is two blocks away. Still, I'm in the mood for crisp vegetables; the taste of something clean. On the way, I think about the letter, wondering what news it might hold; I put my hand over my pocket to protect it. At the store, the vegetables in the boxes outside are browned and sagging, so I don't buy any. The greengrocer shrugs apologetically at me from inside and I send him a little wave.

My apartment is warm but not as heavy as the street. I switch on the air-conditioning; it bangs and thrums, so I switch it off again – one less noise in the city's din. I warm up some tortellini that Vito has given me, but they are dry and salty in my mouth. I drink a cup of milk to loosen up my tongue; it tastes good – cold and creamy like the milk back home. When I've finished eating, I push the window wide and pull my chair up to it. I sit with my back to the window and let the warm air dry the sweat on my blouse. Taking the envelope from my pocket, I slit it open with the blade of a scissors. There is money, of course, and, this time, a photograph. I put the dollar bills into my pocket and study the picture.

There is Mattie, moon-faced and smiling, stouter now than when he left; his arm is draped across the black wife and she is grim and thin, holding a baby across her breasts. Is this a son? My grandson? They are standing at a railing by the sea. There is writing on the back of the picture. I study the curls and squiggles; I see 'M' for Mattie and another 'M'. This is one of the letters I know; I know B makes the start of Bridie too. Maybe, I think, he has named his boy Matthew, for himself.

I unfold the letter: it's a long one, three pages. Poring over each sheet in turn, I run my finger under the lines, trying for letters and words, pushing into my mind for something. When I reach the end of each page, I toss it over my shoulder, out the window, to the street below. I throw the envelope out after the pages and hold the photograph between my fingers; I stare at the three faces and go to send it over my shoulder, along with the rest. My hand stops in mid-air and I look at the photo again; my darling son is smiling for me. I take up the scissors and cut Mattie from the picture. Throwing the other bit of the photograph out of the window, I bend and kiss Mattie's happy face. Next Tuesday I will show Vito a picture of my son.

Poisson d'Avril

*I*t was the portrait that hung beside Madame Henri's door that decreed the type of man I would fall in love with when I grew up. For a time, the man in the painting was the only man I knew. Madame kept an all-female house; my mother and I had a small apartment overlooking rue Copernic. When I was a girl and Maman stopped to gossip with Madame Henri about the other tenants, I would linger in front of the picture. I took in the man's red cloak, the garland of thorns that made a blood-ruby slide towards his long nose, and his eyes with the two points of light in their darkness. He charmed me, that man. I liked to look at him as he liked to look at me. His mournful face was framed by long hair; he held a stick that I thought might be for beating horses or his wife. He was the kind of man you could tell secrets to.

It was Maman who pointed out my uniform taste in men.

'Another seaweedy beard; more solemn eyes,' she said, after meeting Christophe for the first time. 'Madeleine, all your *beaux* look the same.'

I laughed and kissed her face. 'Yes, it is true, Maman.'

'Of course it's true. Have I ever been wrong about anything?' She sipped her coffee. 'Men are gullible creatures, Madeleine, but they own all the power. Remember that.'

I tidied away the cafetière and cups. 'I will be back tomorrow morning, Maman.'

She sighed. 'At least I have the cat to talk to.'

'I'll buy some chocolate fish for you in the *pâtisserie*,' I said. 'You'll like that.'

I went to hug her and she batted me away. 'Leave, leave,' she said.

At the bottom of the stairs I stopped at Madame Henri's door and looked at the portrait.

'*Bonjour, mon roi*,' I said. He stared back, pale and anxious, his knuckles white around the stick. 'Did you know that Christophe troubles me? I give my all to him, body and soul but, on his side, I know I have touched only the glass over the picture. So to speak.' I trailed one finger down the man's nose. '*Au revoir*,' I called, and hurried out onto rue Copernic.

Old Gustave in the *pâtisserie* knocked on the window and blew me a kiss; I waved and ran on. I had to hurry; Christophe was waiting and he hated to wait. I scuttled down to place Victor Hugo and took the métro.

Christophe's room on rue du Marché des Blancs Manteaux smelled, always, of the Seine; that clean, green, slow-moving river stench which is as welcome as air. His door was ajar so that I would know to come in without knocking and he lay under the sheet like a gift ready to be unwrapped. But Christophe, being impatient, tossed back the cover to reveal his naked self with a sly, triumphant smile. I ran to him and kissed his mouth; his moustache itched my nose. Unpeeling me from my skirt and underwear, with a deftness I could never manage, he pulled my body under him and pushed inside me. The pain was ragged but welcome and we moved fast together, his hair falling around my face.

Afterwards, Christophe slept and I enjoyed the white light of his room, snug as a tomb. I watched him, his eyes closed, looking peaceful. He kept himself apart in the bed, cautious even in sleep; he never reached to touch me when we lay together, as if he was afraid I would turn out to be someone else – a wrong someone. He woke, blinking in the brightness.

'How is your maman?' he said.

'She likes to say she's lonely but half the neighbourhood visits her each day.'

'You will never have another mother; be kind to her,' he said.

'I love my maman; I am always kind to her.'

I turned my face from his. At thirty-three, Christophe was twelve years older than me but I hated when he wedged the fact between us with unasked-for advice.

31

'Madeleine, stop pouting,' he said, and popped my lips with one finger. I pushed his hand away.

'What about *your* mother?' I said. 'Are you a good son to her? What's she like?'

'She's a saint.'

Christophe rolled over me and off the bed. He stood and stretched his arms high, making his joints crack. His lean body was pale as a cadaver – blue in its whiteness – and dark hair nestled above his legs and the long stem of his cock.

'When will you take me to meet your mother? You've met mine,' I said, reaching to stroke his thigh.

'There may not be time.'

'What do you mean, Christophe?'

'Nothing, Madeleine. Nothing at all. Of course you will meet her. Come, let's walk up to Montmartre to see what we can see.'

I dressed quickly but still Christophe was ready before me, standing by the door twitching his beard and watching every button I closed; my fingers jammed and fumbled. When I was done he helped me into my coat and we ran down the stairs onto rue du Marché des Blancs Manteaux and turned into the Marais.

Sacré-Coeur went in and out of the fog as we climbed towards it; its bells were stilled for Maundy Thursday.

'The chimes have flown to Rome to see the Pope. Isn't that what you Parisians say?' Christophe said.

'Do we?'

He laughed and kissed me. 'My poor girl.' He gripped my hand and we marched up the steep laneway; I had to skip to keep pace. At the Lapin Agile he paused and turned to me. 'I have to meet someone in here. I'm owed money. Will you wait outside?'

I nodded and stood by the window while Christophe went in. He stopped at a table where a red-haired man was eating. They spoke but Christophe didn't sit; he put his hand on the man's shoulder but the man shrugged him off and continued to fork food into his mouth. The man stopped eating and leered at Christophe; he took a pouch from his inside pocket and tossed it onto the table. Christophe folded his fingers around it and offered the man a handshake but he ignored it. I saw Christophe wince as he turned to leave.

'Who was that man?'

'That was Jude, an old friend. An ex-friend.' He shook the pouch. 'Now we can eat.'

The fog had closed down over rue Lepic like a swathe of linen; the globes of the gaslights burned through it in a way that comforted me. I have always loved how heavy fog removes some of the city's fussiness. Christophe rushed us down the cobbles and into a bistro; he ordered red wine, bread and roast lamb. He blushed after swallowing the first mouthful of wine, as if blood ran through his veins anew, and his muscles untensed. Flocculent light seemed to hover around his body; I blinked to settle my eyes but the blurred aura remained. When the food arrived he bent his head to the plate and muttered a prayer.

I lowered my head too, pretending to do the same. When I looked up Christophe was grinning at me.

'What?' I said.

'It pleases me that you want to please me. That's all.'

'Perhaps I am pleasing myself.'

Christophe kept his eyes on me while unfolding his cutlery from its napkin. 'Promise me you will always be good, Madeleine. You are *so* good.'

'You speak as if we are parting.'

'Live well, *ma petite*, I just want to say that.'

I placed my knife and fork on the table. 'Christophe, are you going somewhere? Do you not like Paris after all?'

'I don't dislike Paris. I care about it, but it doesn't care about me. One way or another I must be in a place that cares. A safe place.'

'But where are you going, Christophe? I don't want you to go.'

'Life is, for me, no more than a problematic waiting room, Madeleine. I feel that I will be leaving soon, no matter what.'

'Life? What are you talking about, Christophe? You're frightening me.'

He laughed. 'I apologise, think nothing of it. My mood is off.' He cut into a piece of lamb and popped it in his mouth.

I stared at him. 'Something nests in you, Christophe. Something I can't get at.'

He shook his head and pointed to my plate. 'Eat, eat!'

I broke my bread and ate it. When we both had our fill we returned to his room and loved each other as if we had never touched before. Christophe rose up before me and I bowed to him; he entered every open part of me and I took in his hard heat until he gasped. We lay in each other's salt for a long time, kissing and whispering our love.

The bells of Notre Dame des Blancs Manteaux woke me in the morning; they were answered by the clang from Saint-Louis-en-l'Île, Saint-Séverin and, soon, the ring of Saint-Sulpice. The churches clanged and pealed their off-beat chorus to each other while the sun fingered through the window and stole across the bed. I looked around the bright room, so sparse and empty; Christophe was not a man for possessions. He slept, his hair like a dark halo on the bolster. I put my head on his chest and he lifted his hand to caress me; a rush of blood, deep as claret, flowed from his palm onto my breast.

Madame Henri was at her door when I arrived home. Christophe had come with me; he stopped to look at the portrait of the man on the wall and frowned.

'I won't stay long, Madeleine,' he said; 'I need to be somewhere.'

I took his bandaged hands in mine. 'I know, Christophe.'

Madame Henri coughed. '*Bonjour*, Monsieur,' she said to Christophe, then turned to me. 'Madeleine, your maman is not well.'

'What's the matter with her?'

Madame tapped her temple. 'She seems confused; she came downstairs in her night clothes this morning.'

'Again? *Ai, ai*, I don't know what is wrong with that woman.'

Christophe took my hand and we rushed up the stairs. I let us in and called out to Maman.

She emerged from her room, holding her head. 'You had no business staying out all night, Madeleine; it was wrong of you.'

'But, Maman, you knew I would be away last night. I told you I was staying with Christophe.'

'Did I? I don't recall.'

I placed a packet of silver-wrapped fish in her hands. 'See, I've bought your favourites: chocolate sardines.'

Maman looked at the *poissons d'Avril*. 'My brain is a sardine today.' She toppled a little and grabbed onto the table. 'My head hurts.'

'Sit, sit,' Christophe said, and he guided Maman back into her room and onto the slipper chair. He sat on Maman's bed and unwound the bandages covering his hands. The cloths were rusted with his blood but when he threw them to the floor and rubbed his thumbs into his palms, I saw that his wounds were gone. I gasped.

'How can this be, Christophe?'

'Shush,' he said, gently, then he stood in front of Maman and laid one hand on her head, the other he placed on his chest. Christophe closed his eyes. 'I am swollen like a wineskin with the love of God,' he said. 'Be well, woman.'

Maman sat in her low chair and swayed a little. She blinked and smiled.

'Madeleine,' she said. 'I feel quite well.'

She laughed and reached for the chocolate sardines I had brought her; unpeeling one after the other from their silver paper, she stuffed them into her mouth like a starving child.

Like everyone else, I suppose, I have always found the change in the seasons wrenching. I had just gotten used to the architecture of the bare trees when the buds came. Suddenly they were more welcome than the stark branches and I marvelled at how they unfolded their tight green hearts and became leaves.

I went into Notre Dame des Blancs Manteaux and lit three candles. Always three, since Christophe told me that to light two was bad luck. I watched their guttering flames: one each for Maman, for Christophe and for me. I thanked God for the spring then left the church and stood under the tree that flanked Christophe's building. I could almost hear the awakening in its limbs. Looking through the grille from the outside door, I saw light flowing down the stairs. I went in and up; the door to Christophe's room was ajar. I pushed it but could tell before I stepped in that he was not there. I stood just inside the doorway. Everything was as it had always been except Christophe's bed was empty and the air no longer smelled of the Seine.

Mother America

' $\mathcal{J}$ come from Fertile, Missouri,' she said, but I didn't believe her. Her car had a bumper sticker that read 'Powered by Jesus'; I didn't believe that either. She had picked me up a few miles outside of Cork city; I'd been hitching for hours with no luck.

'Are you mad, giving a lift to a strange man?' I said, after settling myself into the seat.

'Our Heavenly Father has already made my day,' she said; 'He sent me to make yours. Buckle up.'

'Oh, you're from the God Squad; just my fucking luck.' I looked out at the fields, all yellow and lit-up like childhood, then at her. 'What if I'm a murderer? I could jump you right now.'

'Forbidden fruit makes plenty of jam,' she said, smiling her corny, I'm-in-love-with-the-Lord smile. I looked at her for longer, even though I didn't want to be looking at her. She had that mad hair that some older American women have: a bushy triangle with a fringe like the top of a broom. She grinned a lot.

'Is it not boring being a goody-goody? Don't you ever want to go mental and do something really bad?'

'Such as?' she said.

'I dunno. Maybe something like kicking some annoying bastard like me in the head?'

'Now why in Heaven's name would I want to kick you? I'm a pacifist, for one thing, and I don't *hate* you. I don't hate anybody.'

'You're trying to tell me you don't hate child molesters? Come off it!'

'I pray for them. And their victims.' She smiled straight at me and I could tell there was some more nutsy Jesus-wisdom on its way. 'We all need to pray on the days that end with a Y.'

She put her hand on my knee and squeezed it; my ma used to do that when we drove together in her car. My bloody eyes got all teary. So she wouldn't notice, I leaned forward and examined the Magic Tree that swung from the rear-view.

'"This car is prayer conditioned",' I read and flicked the Magic Tree; its piny smell wafted around. 'What a load of puke. They could have at least written something interesting on it. Like, "Take succour, sucker". Or something.'

She laughed. 'That's real funny. You're a smart young man.'

'Do you know what I hate?' I said, my eyes following the broken white lines down the middle of the road until I felt dizzy.

'Hate's a strong word, son; a strong emotion.'

'What I really *dislike* is dogged positivity; it drains the life out of me.' I rolled down the window, needing air. 'And I'm not your son.'

'So, tell me about your mom.'

'No,' I said, 'I won't.' She swung the car onto the hard-shoulder and sped along it for about fifty metres before braking so fast that my whole body jerked forward; I nearly shat myself. 'What the fuck was that?' I shouted.

She gripped my wrist. 'You listen to me. I said tell me about your mom, so start talking. Start with when she died.'

'How the...? What is this? Is this some kind of piss-take?' I looked around me, for what I don't know. 'Who the hell *are* you?' I asked, pulling at the door handle but it wouldn't open.

'Let's just say I'm your Guardian Angel, sonny.' She let go of my wrist. 'Now talk.'

We sat in silence but I could see she wasn't going to move until I spoke. I sighed, I thought about trying to jump out; I looked at cars and trucks and tractors whizzing by. I rolled my fingers on the dash, glanced at her, then closed my eyes and pictured my ma.

'I could barely stand to visit her,' I said. I glanced sideways at her and she nodded. 'She had that moony face, you know, the way they all look in the end. That was my ma and she was baldy, like a man. And she was bulge-eyed and so bloody tired looking. Even her eyelashes fell out; it made me feel sick to see her. The pains she had made sort of dents all over her face.' I pointed to my forehead and cheeks, then let my hands fall. 'So I left. I went off and didn't tell her I was going. I rang her after a few days and she was confused, you know? Sort of bewildered. I tried to say "I love you" down the phone; it was all I wanted to say, to explain, but the words choked me, they got stuck. It took three more phone calls before I got it out and, even then, I whispered it. "I love you, Ma", I said, but I don't even know if she heard.'

'She heard you, Chris. She forgives you and she loves you.'

'You know my name,' I said, stupidly, then I started to cry. I never cry; I hadn't managed a single tear over my ma until that minute.

The woman leaned over me; her hair swept across my face and it smelled like hay. I half-smiled and went to take her hand, but she opened my door.

'Out now.'

'What?' I said, wiping at the slide of snot and tears around my mouth.

'Out,' she said, gentler this time.

I took my bag from between my legs, threw it out of her car and went to follow it. 'You know my name, at least tell me yours,' I said.

'They call me Mother America,' she said, then she snapped the door shut, and I watched her drive away.

Cri de Coeur

*S*hura's bedroom has her scent, it smells musty and young. Her cheek lolls against my shoulder when I lift her from the bed, but she swoons her head and forces open her eyelids, afraid she will miss something.

'Mummy, are we playing a game?'

'Yes, darling, a new game.' I wonder if she can smell whiskey off me. My edges are dull but somehow I am clear too like water. I carry Shura from her room to the kitchen, her body slack and warm in my arms. 'You must drink this fairy potion, darling, and then we will lie down.'

'On the floor?'

'Yes, my love, here on the floor. See, I've made a cosy bed.'

I hand her the glass and she dribbles the liquid down her throat; she folds her lips against the bitter taste but plays along, settling onto the pillow I have placed on a blanket on the tiles.

'Night, night, Mummykins,' Shura says, her last words to me.

I go to the stove and turn each gas jet to full, then I lie beside her.

*

The trip to Ireland went well. We hired a car in Dublin – an evil-smelling place – and drove west through town after ugly town to Connemara. There the country opens out to the Atlantic like a bride to her groom; it is an untamed, bitterly beautiful place of rock and water. Our hillside cottage was a nearly-ruin on the edge of a rust bogland. But Ted took a leap with his poetry that made everything smooth and bearable. And Sylvia's head did not lie on the pillow between us as it always did at home in England.

The first night we lay tucked in bed, wrapped limb-on-limb around each other to ward off draughts, listening to the sea lashing the shore.

'I can smell dulse,' I said.

Ted sniffed deeply. 'Yes, 'there's a definite tang in the air, I get it too.' His lips brushed my neck. 'Or is it just the tang of you?' He clamped his teeth onto my shoulder and snarled.

'Stop it! You'll wake the children.'

He lay back and I could feel all the unease drain from him; all the bewilderment we shared at how our lives had ended up.

'Ireland will be good to us,' Ted said.

'I think it will.'

The Ireland we had chosen was a land apart; it was a place of reliquaries and bright furze, stone walls and emptiness. Black-faced sheep decorated the roadsides in languid huddles – there were more of them than people. The sea surrounded our headland like a comforting pair of arms.

Irish women, I thought, pretended they didn't want to be noticed but got annoyed when no one paid them any attention. I watched them on the street in Roundstone when we went there and in the pubs. They were dowdy and big-jawed, and seemed to brood. And breed. God, they made babies and the babies were as plain as themselves. Irish men, though, I found handsome in a flinty way.

Every few days I cycled the rutted roadway to the local shop, leaving Shura to play with the others in the garden and Ted writing at the table by the window. The sea spread out beyond the stone walls, shushing like a lullaby, and the Connemara ponies romped, solid and wild, in the fields. The old woman in the shop was called Bríd and she had a grand air of scepticism. Over her dress she wore a dun shop-coat that was radiant with long use.

'There you are,' she would say, when I came through the door, as if I was expected but not altogether welcome. She busied herself tidying the scant display of biscuits, loaves and jars, then disappeared through the strip-curtains to let me browse. The shop

smelled of boiled turnip and some other dense sweet-
ness that I couldn't name. I gathered up whatever I
needed – milk, bread, duck eggs, jam – and Bríd reap-
peared on cue with a resigned, 'Now.'

'Is everything all right beyond?' she said to me one
day, with a flick of her head towards Doonreagan.

'It is,' I said, adopting her speech pattern and
smiling when I caught myself doing it.

'Is something funny?' Bríd asked.

'No,' I said. 'Can I not smile?'

She humphed. 'You can do what you like, Ma'am.'

'We're enjoying the fresh air and the children love
the strand,' I said, to rescue the conversation.

'Ah, the craythurs,' she said, reaching into her
shop-coat and producing three carnival-striped lolli-
pops in twists of plastic. 'For the little ones.'

'You're most kind.'

'There wasn't a child born in Doonreagan House
in a hundred years; it's cursed, you know. Haunted too.'

'We've settled nicely,' I said. 'The only thing both-
ering us is the damp.'

'Well. I'm only saying.' Bríd flicked a cloth over
the counter, then turned her back to me to dust the
shelves. I had been dismissed.

*

I think I would have liked a well-lived life; a simple
life like that of Bríd in the shop. How lovely to know
what each day will bring; how perfect to live in a

steadfast landscape with only the weather to add variety. I am soiled with the grime of all my marriages. Second marriages are always stained by the failure of the first, so what of third marriages and the ones after that? Maybe this is why Ted will not marry me, though any fool can see that the last union – the lifer – is the right one, the one that was meant to be.

The very first time we met, in London, Ted took my hand and said my name, 'Assia'. He didn't mangle it the way most people do; he said it as if he had found a new meaning for it, like Assia was something untouchable that he wanted to caress. Sylvia said my name the way Americans do – like it's another word for snake.

Later, when David and I stayed with them in Devon, I saw that Ted needed the animal, the visceral, the *other*, and that Sylvia had bottled her wildness and become a mushy mother earth. She had painted all their furniture with hearts and flowers, a school-girl-ish impulse, I thought, and she baked and cooked in a way that seemed to beg for praise. She even tried to make me collude with her.

'Assia,' she said; 'come and peel for me.'

'Peel?'

'Potatoes,' Sylvia said. 'You sing for your supper in this house.'

'I never sing,' I said, and walked to the bottom of the garden where Ted and David were collapsed in deck chairs, smoking.

Ted was ripe for plucking, I knew, and I plucked, though I let him believe the first move was his. The note that he left at my workplace a few weeks later

– 'I have come to see you, despite all marriages' – thrilled me; I knew that I had him.

We behaved badly, of course, towards Sylvia and their children; towards my David. Our behaviour was dreadful in general. But what can be said about it all? Love calls some people to act above society, propriety and the whole damn lot. And we suffered mightily for it. I suffer.

But, Ireland. Ireland was our bucolic retreat; our green and rainy oasis away from the London gossips, away from Ted's stagnant parents, and away from Sylvia who was, by then, a ghost.

I was in Ireland before – with David – and hated it. We ate unspeakable food and nearly drowned in the piety of the place: churches everywhere and simple, joyless people. It was in a murky Galway hotel that we decided to separate for good and all: I was to go to Ted; David to Spain. And so we did.

And then Sylvia did what she did and, the day after her death, I lay on her bed in her cold flat, to take a rest, and I listened to the sound of Ted singing 'Waltzing Matilda' to the mourners who had gathered. Knowing Ted, I realised that soon he would be searching for a way to hide, a crevice to slip into and just be. I meant to be that secret place, or at least to go with him to it.

*

Cashel. Ted said it meant 'fortress' in Gaelic. Cashel was our bastion, our happy stronghold. We took the

47

children fishing in the lake over the hill, singing *Row, row, row, your boat* all the way from the cottage to the lakeshore. Shura stayed by me on the bank, pulling at grass, while Ted baited lines for the other two. Shura crawled over and put her head in my lap; I sang into her face, any merry song that came to mind. *Will you go, lassie, go? And we'll all go together, to pluck wild mountain thyme, all around the blooming heather.* I combed her hair with my fingers and kissed her fat little thighs.

'Fatty legs,' I said. 'Miss Fatty Legs!'

She giggled and grinned, showing her snaggly teeth.

The sun was dazzling that day and Ted and the children caught trout. They squealed and were proud showing me the plump, dappled bodies in their sand buckets. I fried up the fish on a campfire and we ate them, even Shura; the sweet, nutty flesh dissolved in my mouth and I can taste it still.

Some days we watched men hump black currachs up from the seashore and the children called, 'The crab men, Daddy. Look, the crab men!' I loved the hookers, with their scarlet sails and elegant dip through the water. I never knew that boats could be things of beauty. The fishermen didn't talk much to us but they gave the children some pieces of sea-glass. These they lined up on the windowsills of the cottage with other beach-combed treasures: whelk shells, striped stones and stray knots of fishing net.

In the pub we drank porter. The locals were gluttonous drinkers and they didn't take to me; I seemed to make them nervous.

'You might be more comfortable out the back,' the landlord would say. Out the back was his wife's parlour and she had a squat collie who frightened me.

'No, I'm happy to stay here.'

'Ho – she wants to be a man,' one old fellow cackled.

The men tried to wheedle more bottles of porter from us but we had no money to spare. Ted loved to chat to them and they liked him, the way people always do; he could talk about the land and about fishing and that was enough for those men.

Bríd in the shop was the only one who spoke to me.

'I need to make a cake,' I said to her one drear March morning as I entered the shop, panting from my bike ride.

'A fruit cake, is it?'

'A chocolate cake. It's my daughter's birthday tomorrow.'

'Eggs, so,' she said. 'Flour. A bit of Stork.'

'A stork? Whatever for?'

Bríd held up a block of margarine with a weary expression; there was a picture of a stork on its gold wrapper. We both laughed.

'Can you bake, Ma'am?' I shook my head and she sighed. 'Come through and I'll show you.'

Bríd tossed an apron over the shop-coat and rolled up her sleeves. She seemed to come alive – a bird taking to the wing after too long on the ground. I watched her sieve and whisk and crack eggs like a dervish while I stood back trying not to feel useless.

Her kitchen was bare but lovely, and I wondered if it was the kind of kitchen my father had known as a boy in Russia – a functional room, oozing cosiness. When the cake was in the range, Bríd made tea and we drank it without talking and listened to the pleasing beat of her pendulum clock. I lifted the teacup to watch its gold rim glint under the overhead bulb.

'Handmade in Galway city,' Bríd said, as if the cup had come all the way from Limoges.

'Is it your wedding china?'

She beamed. 'It is.'

Bríd put Shura's cake in a tin and covered it with a tea-towel; when I took out my purse she refused me.

'Tell your girl happy birthday from Bríd,' she said. 'The little peteen.'

'You're an absolute star.' I kissed her cheek.

She jumped backwards and said 'Oh!' as if I had bitten her. She turned away and grabbed a bar of chocolate from the dresser. 'Melt that and pour it over the cake. Go on with you, now.'

Her face was mottled pink as she waved me off from the door and I balanced the cake tin on the handlebars and wobbled down the boreen.

*

I am lavish with minor qualities. All I am capable of is spinning jingles for advertisements and trying to mother Shura in the best way I can – with love. I wait for Ted to come to us. But he doesn't come. On the telephone we snipe; or he doesn't talk at all and I rant.

He often trots out one of his favourite myths: that at the time of her death, he and Sylvia were soon to reunite. *No, Ted, no,* I want to scream, *you don't remember things well.*

Today on the 'phone he said I am sentimental and demanding, and that I wallow in self-love. I begged him to say something nice. There was silence.

'I can't stop talking and you can't begin,' I shouted. 'Write a verse about that, Herr Poet.' Then I slammed the receiver onto the cradle and sat and cried.

Shura held her doll and stared at me. After a while she sat by me on the tiles and said, 'Poor Mummykins. Darling Mummy.'

*

Back in Ireland I shone, I managed things; I kept the house, I got soil under my nails. The children behaved and we were a family, Ted's little tribe. Still I could never match she who was everything: mother, homemaker, writer, muse. Sylvia floated over our heads all the time we were there, a silent balloon. In Connemara we were waiting and we didn't even know it. And, of course, the inevitable summons came and home to England we had to come. Ted to Devon and his mother's demands; Shura and me to London, out of sight. It was as if time began to move backwards and Ted slipped into his routine of making the same mistake over and again. It's like he enjoys making it or, maybe, if I am kinder, he just can't help himself.

My flat seems to reek with malice; I don't have the energy even to leave it and take Shura out into the air. I feel displaced and unplaceable. One thing I know is that I will not grow old and mad like Wordsworth's Dorothy – a prop in a poet's life. I won't have it. I know what I deserve and what Shura does too, but we don't get what we deserve. We endure. Then we die.

My mind is clotted. Language has no grace now; there is nothing that can be said to mend or re-stitch what has already been sewn into the fabric of us. Ted and I are a flawed garment, ready for the scrap-bag.

So I lift Shura from her bed; her room holds her scent, it smells musty and young. I wonder for a moment if she can smell whiskey off me as I settle her onto the pillow I have placed on a blanket on the tiles.

'Night, night, Mummykins,' Shura says.

I go to the stove and turn each gas jet to full, then I lie beside her.

When I Go Down, Go Down with Me

*H*er husband's breath blankets her lips; his hand rests on her stomach. This is an invitation; he has always been tentative. Can I do this? Máire wonders. The last person he slept with was the girl. Máire thinks 'the girl' but she is twenty-six, so a woman. But she looks young in that stupid way of twenty-somethings, even the clever ones – sort of slack-jawed and incredulous. No, she is the girl after all. Her husband props his shin across hers and groans; Máire realises that he is not awake and probably doesn't know what he is doing. To him, at this moment, Máire's body is the girl's body: fresh, plump and yielding. She witnesses a flash of them together, the girl acrobatic despite her heft, straddling her husband and jigging. Jig-jig-jig.

Máire has never been unfaithful, not since they married, and before that it was just a stray kiss with her sister's boyfriend. There was also the time at the swimming pool where a man had swum up to her and slipped his cock into her bikini bottom and she had let him. She recognised him from the TV and now he is dead. But she hadn't initiated that, so it doesn't count. No, she has never betrayed her husband.

Except sometimes when they make love she thinks of other men; when they *used* to make love, that is. While her husband moved over her, she often thought of her friend's father, the man whose eyes always seemed to be pressed on her, kneading her flesh. His tongue was thin and long, and she was fourteen again and compliant. Her firm buds under his palms. Not the heavy breasts she has now; breasts that fed her daughter and, before that, Brian. Her friend's father was not easy to banish. He had, she feared, formed her with his stack of porn which was left, she now knows, for her and his daughter to browse. Had that girl been safe in that house? Those magazines were packed with firm-bodied, big-haired youngsters, pink in all the right places, licking each other with one wrong-faced eye to the camera. Because they always had skewed faces those girls; porn seemed to attract the ugly-pretty.

Other times, as her husband explored her body, Máire found herself thinking of Brian's friend. Not the handsome one, but the nerd with tender eyes. When he came to the house with Brian – after she had been thinking of him – she couldn't look at the boy, as if he was complicit in the intimacy. Máire never talked to him those times, bar a hello, in case she blushed or, worse, touched him and set off something terrible.

Máire tries to be exemplary because her kids, like all kids, scrutinise everything she does. She has lapses, of course; no one can be perfect all the time. The children see the tipsy cigarettes she smokes at family parties and hate her for it. Her daughter stares at the fag in her hand, sucking the joy from the moment, so that the cigarette feels like a ridiculous prop. Which it is. Each sneaky smoke, Máire knows, is a small grab at youth or freedom or the past.

Her daughter, if she is honest, looks like somebody else's daughter. Sinéad has black hair and eyes as pale as Achill marble.

'How did you get so beautiful?' Máire says, and the girl looks at her mother and shrugs. She hums with secrets, Máire's daughter. But it is her son, Brian, who really counts; he is the one Máire loves the most of anyone.

Her husband opens his eyes and, when he sees he is draped across her, he snatches himself away and glares at Máire as if she lured him. He pauses, clouded with sleep.

'Is it? What day?' He swivels his head to squint at the alarm clock.

'It's half six. Too early to get up,' she says and, in an instant, he is gone, eyes closed, face to the pillow.

It occurs to her that they don't talk about anything anymore other than his situation; the wars convulsing the globe are not mentioned; the health of their elderly mothers; how the children are getting on at school. Every conversation concerns the girl and him. Him and the girl.

Máire knows that she is not the kind of woman that men fancy; she is dour-looking a lot of the time, a thing she cannot help. God or DNA arranged her face in a way that makes people think she is always sad. That one kiss she shared with her sister's chap might have led to more because he, unlike other men, found something attractive in Máire. His eyes lingered on her face, daring her to hold his stare, and his smile was always receptive when he saw her – a smile that lasted longer than was comfortable for Máire. They kissed once in the ladies' loo of a pub and that was it.

The man from the telly had a big cock, which was lucky – or unlucky? – it wouldn't have fit inside Máire's bikini bottom otherwise. He stuck it in and rooted a bit while dabbing at her breasts and staring into her eyes; then he swam away. It was all done in a minute or so, and was as perfunctory as a stranger stopping to pet your dog. Or something. Dead now; a car-crash-for-one. Oh well, she thinks. She had always liked the industrial silver of his hair.

The affair is a secret but Máire tells her sister. Tríona's kitchen is hot and Máire pulls at the neck of her T-shirt and looks out at Tríona's nodding rose bushes.

'It's all hush-fucking-hush, of course,' Máire says. 'Until he decides what he's going to do. He begged me not to tell the kids.'

'Who is she?'

'The PR girl at Whelan's. She's twenty-six. And dough-cheeked, like someone newly pregnant.' Máire prods at her own cheeks.

'She's not pregnant, is she?'

'Well, she's a bit of a pudding, so it would be hard to tell.'

Tríona tuts; she doesn't approve of fat people. 'And it's definitely over?'

'He says it is but he doesn't seem to know what he wants.'

'And you?' Tríona says. 'What do you want?'

'Well, part of me would like to go asleep and never wake up. Other times I want to clatter him on the jaw with the iron, for being so fucking head-meltingly inconsiderate.'

Tríona flicks the switch on the kettle. 'I wouldn't mind only I was always jealous of you two. You were so *together*. Unassailable.'

'I keep that fact strong in my mind. What else can I do?'

Máire doesn't tell Tríona that her husband wants to go on with the affair as much as he wants to be forgiven, or that she sees him smile when he mentions the girl's name. The smile is involuntary like a wave that ripples in the wake of a boat. And she doesn't mention the Chinese lantern her husband and the girl sent skyward together either.

They lit and let it off from the Millennium Bridge. He looked so genuinely moved by the relating of this story that Máire was shocked into a trance of listening. She submitted to the charm of the scene: the two lovers on a bridge; the red lantern glowing and floating; river gushing, revellers rushing. Her husband's voice rolled over her and his dripping tears even kindled a sort of pity in her.

The girl invented this romantic interlude; the modern version of pinning hope to a rag tree with a scapular or hair ribbon; some innocent, personal object to make one of two. Maybe Máire underestimated the girl's power. She was clever to use a ritual to settle herself under his skin; her husband was a man for rituals. Yes, how smart the girl was, how *young*.

'She has a PhD,' her husband said.

Máire hooshed herself back from her thoughts and stared at him. Why was he telling her this stuff exactly? Oh yes, it was part of the regret. The affair was over – he had finished it – and he was sad and confused. Doing the right thing did not sit as well as he'd hoped. Máire was amazed at his capacity for ignorance, for selfishness, for causing hurt.

'Educated,' Máire said. 'Well.'

Tríona clinks teacups and saucers, lays out a feast of scones and jam. Máire can see that her sister is biting back the bulk of her annoyance. There is a lot she could say.

'The age of him; he'd want to cop onto himself,' Tríona says eventually, pouring tea.

'He has copped on. He will.' Máire heaps sugar onto her spoon. 'She's from Donegal you know,' she says glumly.

'Oh. That accent.' Tríona sits and stares at Máire, discussion stalled.

Máire has found herself, lately, jealous of young people. It is not that she is old – fifty is not *old* nowadays – but she feels grumpy about the accomplishments of the younger women she sees, about their confidence. Those prodigiously able seventeen-year-olds who turn up on TV talent shows. How do they manage to accumulate all that perfection over such a short time span? What are their parents doing that has eluded her? Máire acknowledges her children as undistinguished, though a little extraordinary in their own way, maybe, just because they are hers. But they are not publicly successful, not point-in-the-street beautiful like the kids on TV, with their quirky faces and amazing voices.

The jealousy of course is about more than talent – it's about money. These youngsters have so much money. She and her husband, though rarely poor, always seem to lag behind their friends, who can suddenly install a new kitchen, or fly to Australia for three weeks. The most expensive holiday they managed was a week in Corsica and Máire didn't enjoy it; the kids were young then and they had left them with Tríona. Máire missed them viciously. And Corsica was hot, so cloyingly hot that they were too languid even to make love, so there was no extra closeness to toy with during the day; no anticipation of the night. It put her off foreign countries.

Máire sits in the kitchen, mulling over a conversation she had with Sinéad the night before. Her daughter is reactive, headstrong; she collects lame ducks and is always ready to fight for them. These days her father is her cause.

'Why are you so hard on daddy all the time?' Sinéad said.

'I don't know what you mean.'

'He asked if you wanted to open a bottle and you snorted. That was your answer – to snort like a pig.'

'We're going through a patch, Sinéad. Things are a bit hard but we'll be grand.'

'You could try to be nice to him; that would be a start.'

'I'm as nice as I can be at the moment.'

'Huh,' Sinéad said, and stalked off, infuriated, Máire knew, by her calm. If only Sinéad knew.

We'll be grand, Máire thinks, sweeping crumbs off the table into her hand then piling them back up. Sweep and pile; a hillock of crumbs to arrange and re-arrange; it could go on for a long time. We'll be grand, grand, grand, she thinks. Of course we will.

Brian comes crashing through the back door with a face like thunder; he thumps the wall and screeches from deep in his throat.

'Brian! Take it easy,' Máire says. 'What's wrong?' She glances at the clock. 'Why are you home?'

'I didn't go to school today, Mam; all right?'

'Well, where *did* you go?'

'Bray.'

'Bray? I don't get it. Why did you go there?'

'I was on the hop, Mam; OK?'

'Brian.' Máire is genuinely surprised. Why is her son, of all people, mitching from school?

'I saw Dad there.'

'Dad?'

'In Bray. He was with someone. He was kissing the fucking face off her, Mam, in broad daylight. On the prom!'

'Oh.' Máire sits at the table and taps her fingers, like someone in need of a song. Brian stamps up the stairs to his room.

This time her husband has poked a hole in the sacred memories of her heart. They had spent their honeymoon in Bray; two late bloomers giving love a go. The place had a lunar pull on them – it was where they went, in sickness and in health, for anniversaries, for birthdays, and on outings with the children. Their honeymoon hotel still faced the bay, its paint ravaged from the wind but still friendly-looking, like a benevolent aunt. *Welcome*, it always seemed to say, *welcome back; I remember you.*

For Máire, Bray was the mile-long tip along the promenade; it was the cliff walk to Greystones, arms around each other; it was the shell-dappled trinket box he had bought her to hold her rings in at night; it was a paper twist of salty periwinkles poked from their shell with a pin; it was her first real taste of wine, her first real taste of him. It was kissing on the prom

61

in broad daylight because they were married people and nothing or no one could stop them.

Máire wonders now if the Chinese lantern had actually been launched from Bray and not from a bridge over the Liffey as he'd said. She pictures it, the prom empty at dusk save the two of them, him and the girl; the fumble with matches; the lantern rising up above Dublin Bay, orange and light over the water. The hotel settled benignly behind them, approving, as always, of new beginnings.

They had sworn when they married that if one of them wanted out, the other would let them go easy. There would be no questions or recriminations; no weepy scenes. It was a bargain made in the giddiness of their early days when such a thing was unfathomable. No one would be leaving! Now she tries to remember who suggested the pact in the first place. Had he? How foolish we were, she thinks, to make a promise like that; how unrehearsed on the snares of love. No, I will not let him go easy, Máire thinks, I will not let him go at all.

Taking a bottle of wine from the rack and one glass, she sits in the kitchen and waits, wondering if she will do this kind of waiting again, or if this will be the last time. How do you right a toppled marriage? Get it back on its feet and teetering forwards like a splay-legged foal, newborn and unsure. Maybe, Máire thinks, the legs of this marriage are too gnarled and it will never be steady again. She uncorks the wine and pours. Around her the house sighs and creaks, then sighs again, answering itself back.

Moon Hill

A cotton-ball moon hangs over Knocknarea. I push a wider gap in the curtains and stare up at it, before turning back to Oisín's cot. I lean over the rail and scoop his breath to my nose; it is luxuriously sweet – the lovely, frightening smell of sick baby. I am so glad that Oisín, like my other three sons, was born at night. That way, all of them have the gift of seeing *na daoine maithe* – the good people – who will keep them safe. Superstition and its imagined cures have always kept me light. I know that charms are probably as useless as a fresh poultice on an ancient wound, but I cling to them anyway. I never cut my fingernails on Sundays; I jump in the path of black cats; I pluck luck-pennies from the ground; I place a blade of hay from each year's crib in my purse; and I don't bring lilac indoors.

I lean over Oisín and unfurl the collar of his babygro. He is my last straw child; the marriage fixer. I was hoping for a girl but it was not to be; Cormac didn't care either way. Oisín sleeps. I go back to the window to look at the moon. Its pale coin suspended over the hill is a comfort and I decide that by morning Oisín will be better. For me. For himself. And for Regina, who will arrive tomorrow, expecting order.

Regina steps off the train and walks the platform ahead of a gaggle of businessmen. With her red hair and blue coat she is like a kingfisher blazing through fog.

'Audrey,' she calls, waving her arm over her head, though she is feet away. She skitters up and we hug tightly. Regina dips her head to Oisín in his buggy. 'How's my baby dumpling? It's your favourite auntie.'

'Your only auntie,' I say. 'He's not well at the moment. He has a tummy upset.'

'He'll be grand, won't you, pet? Better before you're twice married and once a widower. Remember granny used to say that?' She prises my fingers from the buggy handles and flounces ahead a few steps. 'Look at me – I'm Audrey Fitzperfect.'

I trundle behind, pulling her trolley case. A single magpie swoops into the station and lands on a girder; it beaks the air and twitches while looking around, as if waiting for something. I stop and salute it madly, hoping its twin will arrive and sit beside it.

Regina carries on towards the exit and I have to jog
to catch up.

In the morning we drive down to the sea at Strandhill
and park by the golf links. It is cold and fresh but
there are lots of people out walking; it is the first
sunny day of the autumn. A fisherman on the sand
path takes one look at Regina's hair fluttering from
under her cap and turns away from us, his face grim.
I want to tell him she is a henna redhead but he has
seen her now and his day's fishing is ruined. I watch
him return to his car and pack away his rod and tackle.
Lately, my dreams have been swimming with fish; fer-
tility and fish are always bedfellows.

Like most childless women, Regina enjoys the
chance to push a buggy, to claim the baby for her
own. She pulls down the rain-covers to protect Oisín
from the wind and my arms feel light and useless as
I walk along beside her; I plunge my hands into my
jacket pockets. Cormac has taken our older boys away
for the day, to give me time with my sister. There
are wet-suited surfers like overgrown tadpoles on
the strand, getting instruction before they go into
the water. The sea foams with enough breakers to
make surfing worthwhile. At the rocky approach to
the beach, I take Oisín from the buggy and park it
behind a boulder.

'Here, give him to me,' Regina says, and I hand
over my son, watching while she carries him away;
she kisses his face and murmurs into his ear. The
rocks wobble under her feet.

'Be careful,' I say, but my words are thrown back to me by the breeze.

I placed half an onion under Oisín's cot last night and he has not thrown up since. Cormac hovered beside me in the boys' bedroom while I slipped the saucer with the onion onto the floor, pushing toys and books out of the way.

'What are you doing? The smell of that will make him even more queasy,' he said.

'It works.'

'Says who? Oh, don't tell me, it's one of your granny's "cures".'

'What if it is?' I said. 'Do you not want him to get better?'

Cormac tutted and went back along the bungalow's corridor to where Regina was drinking tea by the sitting-room fire.

Regina has Oisín by the hand and they are stop-starting along the beach. He is new to walking and is not sure if it is something he likes. I catch up with them and see that Oisín's hat has lodged on his ears, bending them and making him look elfish. My love for him burbles into my throat and I want to catch him in my arms and feel his small, wielding body against mine. But Regina is playing mammy today and here she is with a stick, carving his name into the sand by the lacy shoreline, spelling out each letter for him.

'O-I-S-Í-N. Oisín. Isn't that great?'

She gives him the stick and lets him poke in the sand. I take a whip of bladderwrack in my hand and waggle it for Oisín to see.

'Look, baba.'

He glances at the wrack. 'Ush,' he says, his version of his name, then turns back to where Regina crouches and points at the letters in the sand. I drop the seaweed and watch the tide nudge it and retreat; nudge, retreat.

'Cormac is having an affair,' I say.

Regina's head whips up and she shields her eyes. 'How do you know?'

'I'm not stupid, Regina.'

She stands, saddles Oisín onto her hip and strides towards Culleenamore Bay; she stops to let me come level with her.

'Are you sure?'

'I found a hotel receipt; so fucking predictable.' I laugh.

'Have you talked to Cormac? Told him you know?'

'Not yet. I'm hoping he'll just get it out of his system. I'm OK with it, as long as he doesn't leave us.'

'He wouldn't leave the boys,' Regina says, fixing Oisín's hat over his ears. 'Will we go on or go back?' she says, more to the baby than to me.

*

I cut a cross in the bread before putting it into the oven. The lunar haze over Knocknarea draws my eye up to Queen Maeve's cairn as I stand at the sink. From this distance, the cairn looks like the plunger on the desk bell of the hill. Up close it is a ten-metre high mound of rocks. Maeve had a wayward husband or two, I think, and a clatter of sons; but she also got the daughter she wanted.

I turn to face the dining table. My sister and my husband are playing cards, silently turning aces and spades, trying to bluff each other.

'Would you like to walk up Knocknarea tomorrow, Regina, to see Maeve's cairn?'

She glances at Cormac before answering. 'Sure.'

'The boys can come with me to Sligo,' Cormac says. 'Oisín too.'

'Great,' I say, and start to set the table for dinner. They move their card game to the sitting room and I hear the low thrum of their laughter and chat through the wall.

The track is rocky to begin with and deep ruts from tractors have hardened in the cold; cow pats are littered everywhere. We are ginger over the stones but soon the path turns to a mud trail and the going is easier. I stop before we reach the stile.

'Let's pick our stones to add to the cairn before we go any further,' I say. 'You're meant to carry your stone up the hill.'

I choose a fist-sized rock with wormy holes; it must have found its way from the beach. Regina's one is lavender and smooth, like a goose egg.

'Can we sit for a minute?' Regina says, and we perch side by side on a grass bank.

I point down to the bay. 'Look, you can see the quarry at Ballysadare.'

Regina slumps forward and holds her head in her hands. 'Urgh,' she says, pushing the noise, it seems, from her stomach to her throat.

'Are you OK?' I rub her back.

'Queasy, that's all.'

'You must have caught Oisín's bug.'

'I'm grand. Come on.' She stands and stretches; I see that her face is pallid.

'You look really sick, Regina. We'll go back. It gets steep after this.'

'I want to go to the top.'

The path is worn from footfall at the steepest sections, making it almost like steps. Still it is tough going. Regina pants as she climbs beside me and her nose runs. When the cairn comes into view she stands suddenly, leans forward and vomits. I wait for her to stop heaving, then mop her mouth with tissues. I make her lie on the grass beside the path, with my scarf for a pillow.

'We should have turned back.'

'If I didn't come up here now, I'd never come,' Regina says.

I look at Queen Maeve's cairn, stretching above us, rock on rock, and I imagine her inside, armour-clad, standing to face her enemies. Fearless Maeve. Regina hands me her stone but stays lying down.

'Put it on for me, will you?'

I walk to the cairn. 'Maeve, I'm putting two stones on your cairn,' I say, as I add them. 'One for me, one for my sister. Send us your strength and protection.'

I go back to Regina. She is sitting up, watching me approach; the wind lifts her hair around her eyes.

'Audrey,' she says.

I lift my hand. 'Don't say anything. I realised last night. If it's you, I know he won't leave us.'

'But, Audrey…'

'Please, Regina. Let's just get back to the house. You need to go to bed and rest.'

Fish skim and burble through my dreams all night long, as effortless as acrobats. I lunge and try to grab their slick bodies but I can't catch hold of any of them. In the morning I hear Regina throwing up in the bathroom. Cormac lies on his back beside me, staring at the ceiling.

'My only hope is,' I say, 'that she doesn't have a girl.'

My husband turns on his side, away from me and, through the bedroom window, we both watch the sun rise over Knocknarea.

Triangle Boy

The Asch Building rose so high it seemed to tickle the clouds. You stood outside, head thrown back to look to the top, thinking you'd never get inside. But in you went and flounced into the elevator as if you'd been riding one all your life, instead of what you were used to, which was climbing a ladder into the attic of a Dublin cottage. Jaysus, it was ripe inside that box; the smell of dirty armpits and hot feet made you weak but, still, it was brilliant. It shot up to the tenth floor, leaving your head and stomach below on Greene Street. You were the only boy. The elevator belched you out with a scatter of girls who, like yourself, were starting at the Triangle that day. In the time it took to get to the top you had made a friend. Gae was from Italy and sixteen, same as you; her eyes were black as a rook's. When you stepped out of the elevator, Gae breathed out quickly.

'Oh, I do not like to be up high,' she said.

'You're all right,' you said. 'Couldn't be safer.'

You were met by a woman called Talya; she gave each of you a brown apron to put on. 'The price of this garment will be deduct from your first pay,' she said.

Deducted, you wanted to say but you didn't dare. Talya's apron was white; the only one that was. She stood staring at you all, so you slipped on the aprons and Gae had to help you with the strings on yours.

The black elbow of a Singer sewing machine topped table after table in the big room; they buzzed like jackhammers as girls and women fed cloth through them at speed. *Tu-te-tu-te-tu-te-tu-te* they went; the noise of hundreds of them filled your head. One of the women looked up to see who Talya had brought in; the rest kept sewing as if you were vapours. Talya called the woman out by pointing at her.

'Keep your head down,' she roared, into her face, then shoved her back towards her Singer with short hand-stabs, the same way you'd push a goat along a road.

'Will we use one of those machines?' Gae asked.

'*Nyet*,' Talya said, snorting a laugh, 'they are for proper workers. You will sort rags.'

She placed you and Gae opposite one another in a back room and showed you how to bind scraps for the ragman. Each bundle was fifty or so off-cuts and you had to tie it into a tight parcel with strips of cloth. The worst remnants – the bits that were stained with oil from the buckets by the machines – were to be thrown into the rag bin.

'Behave yourselves in here; keep your mind to your work. I will be back often,' Talya said, and she left, pulling the door tight behind her.

You frowned. 'That Talya's an old bag,' you said.

'Old bag,' Gae said, giggling. 'Old rag!'

The two of you laughed and looked at the enormous piles of material in the small room; they spilled from the table and from wicker baskets; they were stacked in front of the windows, blocking out the light. You shrugged at each other and began to work.

'Seán, tell me about Ireland.' Gae was sorting rags but she looked up and her eyes on you were kind. She was neatly made, slender, the sort of girl you might like to put your arm around and walk with through the park.

'What's to tell?'

'I would like to know about your family.'

So you told her about your ma and her lovely voice, how she sang to you all every evening as you lay under the eaves, the words drifting up like wood smoke from her spot beside the fireplace, until you fell asleep. You told her how Big Jim Larkin was fighting for the Irish workers.

'But I couldn't find a job, so I took the cattle boat to England; I came to America from there. I'm going to earn pots of money for my ma. And to make sure my brother Danny takes the boat after me.'

'My sister and me left our village together,' Gae said. 'It is a place for the nearly dead; every young person leaves. But New York is so dark; I did not know it would be this way. I walk down to the river to feel the sun on my face.'

That day at the garment factory passed quickly and the days following it too; Gae was sweet company and you took to eating together, side by side on the rag-room floor. She would share the spicy Abruzzese sausage she liked, and you would hand her a piece of the flatbread you bought from the Jewish man on the street. Gae called these 'two-cent lunches'.

'I will eat in a restaurant some day,' she liked to say, 'with silver forks and crystal glasses.'

You imagined yourself there with her, spivved up in a tweed suit.

Evenings and Sundays you spent alone, trawling the avenues, your face always tipped upwards. How did the skyscrapers stay standing, windows stacked row on row, on and on, high up into the air? Whose idea was it to clutter all the buildings together like stands of trees blocking out the sky? You thought of Dublin, the way Sackville Street was so wide and flat; the highest thing there was old Nelson on his perch. The light fell down that street with ease, fat golden beams of it in summer, and the trams had plenty of space to glide in and out to Kingstown and Howth. In New York the sun skimmed along the tops of the buildings like a stone across water and the streets were made narrower by shadows and traffic. All the world seemed to jostle through the city and it frightened you at times.

You missed birdsong; the chorus each morning that woke you at home and the calls the birds made to each other all day. You and your brothers would set box-traps for the birds, lying for hours in sodden grass to pull a string and catch them under the box, hoping to make pets of them; it never worked but you did it week after week anyway, always optimistic, always patient. No bird sounded outside your Lower East Side window; you woke to the snoring and farting of the other boys and men packed into the room, and to bells, engines and horses' hooves outside.

You looked for birds. Every tree you saw, you lingered underneath it, ears straining for cheeps and chirrups. When you found birds in a park they were different, too odd to make you feel at home. The American robin was a bloated, ugly thing compared to the ones in Dublin; the New York robin would have swallowed two Irish ones whole and fit a third in his belly for luck. And he chirped as if asking a question, the same one over and again: *When will you leave me? When will you leave me? When will you leave me?*

You missed your ma too, the way she relied on you and told you how strong you were, how helpful. It would have done you good to see her face. You craved the slack heat of her body; if she could have held you against her, just the once, you would have felt safe.

Six days a week, your lives were wrapped around the Triangle. It was overcrowded and hot, and the doors and windows were locked from the outside – to stop people leaving during work, they said – but

when the likes of Talya was not around, there were
laughs to be had. Some of the boys sang bawdy
songs, or a girl dressed up in a yard of cloth, pretending to be a nun or a beggar. You and Gae were
as close as sister and brother, always minding each
other; always with your heads bent together, telling
stories.

'Because I'm here, I won't be on the new census
back home,' you said to Gae. 'It'll be like I don't exist;
I might as well be a corpse.'

'Perhaps your mother will write your name in,'
she said.

'She might,' you said, but you knew your ma was
filthy with honesty and wouldn't like to do the wrong
thing.

Gae told you her father was killed in an earth-
quake and his body was never found.

'Since then *mia madre* sits by the town bridge,
waiting for him to cross it.' She shook her head. 'It
was like living with two ghosts.'

Every Saturday morning, first thing, Gae sang
out, 'Pay day, Seán!'

'Don't I know it, girl,' you replied, thinking of
the couple of quarters you would call your own, once
you had stuffed the envelope for posting home. Gae
was going to help you choose a shirtwaist to send to
your ma, when you had saved up enough spare dimes.

Talya tried to separate the two of you. 'You talk
too much, not enough work.'

Gae threw down her rag bundle and marched up
to the misters' office. 'I will go in, Talya. I'll tell them

about your smoking den if you don't leave me and Seán alone.'

Talya and some of the other women spent ages each day in a back room where they went to gossip. The trails from their cigarettes wafted under the doorway, and, when the door opened and they came out, it was like a train engine had puffed its steam into the room. Gae stood with her hands on her hips and the sewing machines nearby slowed then stopped. When Talya saw she had an audience, she said 'Uck,' and stalked away. For all her strutting, she hated a proper fight.

You never caught sight of either of the misters; it was only after the trial you saw them, on the front of the *New York Times*. In the picture, Mr Blanck looked as if he had just heard a joke, but Mr Harris's face showed that he didn't want any jokes; he agitated a pair of gloves through his hands. No wonder he was spooked; he knew they were guilty, though the judge said they had broken no law.

You and Gae parted each evening on Washington Place. That Friday in March you watched her walk away, her dark skirt hiding her legs – legs that you imagined were soft but firm. If only your fingers could slide up them into the soft cave at the top; if only you could unbutton the shirt at her throat and caress her neck, gently. Gae turned and waved, sending a jump to your balls.

'*Arrivederci*, Seán,' she called, '*arrivederci*.'

'*Slán*, Gae,' you said, using the only word of Irish you knew; a word to send her safely back to her room in Mulberry Street. 'See you tomorrow.' Your face was scalding but you waved and she turned and walked on.

You doubled back down Greene Street. Easter was three weeks away; you would ask to spend Easter Sunday with Gae and her sister. You were sure she wouldn't mind; it was only a matter of putting it the right way, an invitation not a request. You couldn't bear to spend the day alone, marching up and down the avenues like a gobdaw. Your ma, you knew, would get Mass with all the children alongside her and then she'd make something eggy for them afterwards: soda bread with raisins, if she could manage it, or drop scones.

Gae came into the back room lilting a tune; pay day had come around again and the next day was Sunday which meant leisure.

'Would you like to spend Easter Sunday with me?' you blurted out, before she had even sat. 'You and your sister.'

Gae grinned and nodded. She placed her two hands on your shoulders and she was so close you could smell her breath; it was girlish, sugary.

'We could take a picnic to the park,' she said, as if she had already planned it.

She pulled the pins from her hat with both hands and you saw how her breasts pushed forward. You wanted to gather her to you and hold her; your eyes wouldn't crawl from her face.

'Seán?' Gae said, and stepped back.

You could feel the scarlet rise in your neck and cheeks, so you bent and grabbed rags from the pile by your chair. Gae laughed; a gentle, fizzing sound that wrapped around your heart in comfort.

'We'll have the Easter to beat all Easters,' you said, bending yourself to the work.

'*Sì, sì*. We will,' Gae said.

It wasn't until grey smoke puffed in under your door that you knew something was wrong. The fire must have been going for a while before you realised what was happening. Yes, you heard shouting, but people often bawled each other out on the main floor. You were tucked inside the rag room, heads down, doing what you were meant to be doing.

'Come on, Gae,' you said, grabbing at her arm and she dropped what she was working on.

You pulled open the doors to screaming and hurrying footfall; the usual clamour of machines was gone. Flames lapped, then rushed across the sewing tables and smoke plumed from every part of the room. The heat was immense, like a turf fire that had been burning for days with logs to help it on. A gushing noise rose above everything, resembling nothing you'd ever heard in your life; people ran past you, batting at flames with swatches of cloth. Rag bins popped and exploded, sending blue fire leaping to the ceiling. You dragged Gae towards the elevator. A girl screeched something in Italian at Gae.

'What'd she say? What'd she say?'

'The elevators have shut down. The stairs. Go!'

We rushed to the stairwell but there was already a swarm of people piling down the steps. You could see that the doors at the bottom were still locked from the outside and a great jam of girls was crushed against them; some of them tried to stick their fingers into the gap to prise open the doors but, of course, it was useless. The heat was sickening; it pressed on your nose and mouth along with the smoke. You both coughed and coughed. Everyone was hacking hard; some held cloth across their mouths.

'Jesus Christ almighty.' You dragged Gae back from the stairwell; her eyes were hooded and she seemed to shrink as you looked at her. People were screaming and shoving into you; everyone was gasping for air. 'Up, Gae. We have to go up on the roof.' You pointed and she shook her head.

'No, no. I cannot go there.'

'It's our only chance.'

You knew the way to the roof; you'd often gone there to smoke a cigarette and look at the comings and goings on Greene Street. You would salute the fellas smoking on the roof of the next building and it made you feel like the king of New York, sitting up there above the din. You pushed Gae ahead of you but she was small and people were bashing against her as they ran past, looking for a way out. Talya careened into Gae and you grabbed her by the arm.

'Follow me, Talya.'

But her eyes were blank and she shrugged you off. She was muttering in Russian, something that sounded like a prayer. You dragged Gae behind you up the steps to the outside; mercifully the door was unlocked and you burst out into the cold, gasping. You both collapsed on the rooftop and sucked air into your lungs; Gae spluttered and coughed. You spat out the dirty taste in your mouth.

The fellas from the next building whistled and held their hands out to you. 'We'll drag you across, come on, come on,' they yelled.

The space was wide – a few yards – but you saw that it could be done. You shoved Gae ahead of you but she dodged back.

'I cannot,' she wailed. 'I cannot; it's too high.'

You pulled her to you and shook her. 'Gae, you have to. We have to, it's our only chance.'

'No,' she whispered, 'I cannot.'

Gae leapt from your arms and ran back across the roof and down the stairs. You went after her and tried to catch her. She pulled away from you and dashed down the corridor.

'Gae, Gae!'

'*Arrivederci*, Seán,' she called, '*arrivederci*.' And she disappeared into the smoke.

The fireman had big ears; they flopped forward like a dog's. 'You're OK, son. I've got you.'

'I must have passed out,' you said, embarrassed you'd been lost for a while. Had you been calling out? You'd felt like you were being jogged high on people's shoulders, as if you'd won something. And your ma was there, at the side of the boreen. While everyone else cheered and carried you along, your ma stood and smiled. You put out your hand and called her, but she turned and disappeared into a crowd of people. 'Ma', you called, 'Ma!' It was then that your eyes opened to see the fireman leaning over you. You were sitting on cobbles and there was a meaty stench in the air.

'The smoke made you faint,' he said, and it was only then you realised he was holding you up by the arms and you were swaying like a drunk. 'But you're back, son. You're back.'

'The nets are broken,' somebody shouted. 'Don't jump. Don't jump!'

The cry was taken up all around you; the fire-man leapt away and you swooned backwards, your head landing not on cobblestones but on something soft. You turned over on your stomach and saw that there were bodies lined up against the wall, most of them covered with a bolt of grey material; arms and legs stuck out at cocked angles. The shouts of 'Don't jump' went on and on around you and they were followed by muffled thumps. You looked up and saw dark bundles hurtling from the top of the building, burning as they fell. Down, down they came, like crows shot out of the sky. One hit the cobbles beside you with a thud that turned your bowels to liquid. You looked up again. Girls were screaming at the windows, thumping each other out of the way to get space to crawl onto the sill and jump.

The fire ladders went only to the sixth floor; they propped uselessly against the building while all around people sailed past before hitting the ground.

Every time a body landed, someone ran to them, to see if they were still breathing and to give them a hand to hold before they left.

The firemen's nets had been torn by falling bodies and the water hoses were limp; fire engine horses whinnied and stamped their hooves. You stood up to watch, unable to turn away. Another woman appeared on a window ledge; her white apron shone even against the flames that soared behind her. Before you could move or cry out, the woman blessed herself and jumped. Her skirt cracked and whipped as she fell, beating the air like a wing that would not work.

'Talya,' you whispered and, then, 'Gae.'

Her name caught in your throat like a hook and you put your hands to your face and let sobs shudder through your body. Red water ran by your feet; you got up and went to where Talya lay. Her eyes were open so you pressed the lids down with your fingers; they were warm. Kneeling on the street beside her, you softly spoke an act of contrition into her ear, '*Deus meus, ex toto corde paenitet me omnium meorum peccatorum…*' You crossed her hands on her breast and covered her with your jacket.

You turned your back to the Asch Building and headed down Greene Street.

'Son,' you heard someone call. 'Son!' You looked back; it was the fireman. 'Where are you going?'

You shook your head, turned and walked on. Your feet lead you onto Washington Square and then up Fifth Avenue. The big stores' windows were dressed for Easter with painted eggs in beds of straw and bonnets with yellow bows. People stared at you when you passed and you checked your reflection in a window; your jacket was gone, of course, it was now a makeshift shroud for Talya. You were in your shirtsleeves and when you peered closer you could see that your face was streaked with black.

You walked on and on up the island until you reached the park. You sat under a tree and closed your eyes; a robin's song beat down on your head from above: *When will you leave me? When will you leave me? When will you leave me?*

The Doora Spinster

We were up on Doora Hill, tossing our hankies into the air. I had taken off my skirt and blouse and Dónal was in his pelt, bouncing over the heather, letting the wind take his hanky, then running to grab it back.

Jack Gillespie, our neighbour, was footing turf on the bog. He saw us, laughing and half-dressed, and went to tell our mother. She had sent us with a lemon cake to Miss Madden, who was known as The Doora Spinster, and we had eaten half of it.

Miss Madden let us into her cottage.

'Tell your mother I'm grateful,' she said, inspecting the broken end of the cake. 'There are mighty mice on Doora Hill; they'd take the bit out of your mouth,' she said.

We sat at Miss Madden's table, tickling her cat with our feet, and drinking milk with slices of the lemon cake.

Jack was still in our kitchen when we got home. He pointed at us, saying 'Ooh, ooh' so we'd know we were in trouble.

'They ate the bitch, Missus, I seen them,' Jack said. He called everything 'the bitch'. 'But worse than that, Missus, they were half-undressed. Half-*nude*.' He poked his tongue over his lips.

'That's enough now, Jack', Mammy said, guiding him to the door. She gave him a coin for tobacco and he went off shout-singing, 'Asshole, Asshole, A soldier I will be…'

Mammy tutted. 'You'd no business eating that cake.' But she went delicate on us because Daddy was coming home that night for a week and it made her happy to lie in his arms late in the morning.

The next day, with Mammy and Daddy still wrapped together in bed, we went up Doora Hill to fish our favourite spot on the Dooyertha. It was a fine day.

'We'll swim instead,' said Dónal.

We were about to jump from the riverbank when we saw Jack Gillespie come out of Miss Madden's cottage.

'He'll tell on us again,' I said.

Jack came towards us and we saw that he had no trousers on, just his shirt. His legs were the colour of buttermilk and the shirt was stained brown. He looked dazed and walked right past us.

'Jack,' Dónal called. 'Jack Gillespie! Don't you tell our mammy we were going in the river.'

He turned to us; his face looked queer and sad. He pointed to Miss Madden's house. 'I killed the bitch,' he said. 'She's dead in the bed.' He sat on the riverbank.

We pulled on our clothes and ran home. I knocked on the bedroom door and Daddy roared, 'Go away.'

Dónal said, 'Something bad's happened to Miss Madden.'

'Sacred heart of Jesus,' Mammy whispered when we told them what Jack had said. Daddy leapt out of bed and ran up the hill to Miss Madden's.

Jack was sent to the asylum in Dublin and our daddy moved back home, so we were a real family again. Mammy called it a blessing in disguise.

When the Hearse Goes By

*M*y brother's widow, Ivy, lived in Paris. I went there to sympathise with her, though I liked neither her nor him. Bernard was buried in Père Lachaise before I left Cork. I planned to visit his grave, to stand and look at it, to see where he was deposited and, maybe, say a prayer. Mostly to honour our dead mother's rampant religiosity.

I arrived aeroplane-weary at Ivy's door and, when she opened it, the first thing I noticed was her skin, puce from sunburn. On her chest, tattooed in white, were the letters of her name; strangely, the shape of the word sitting under her clavicle was like an ivy leaf. She was a stumpy woman with a man's haircut and down-turned lips that made her look dissatisfied; Ivy didn't ask for that mouth, I knew, but it added to her uncharm.

Her greeting hug was warm. '*Bienvenue*, Fergus. How was your flight?'

'You got burnt,' I said.

'I fell asleep by the river.' She patted her chest. 'Bernard would kill me if he saw it.'

'Bernard so conscientious. Really?'

Ivy snorted. 'Bernard was fussier than an old sow.' She laughed. 'A sow in an apron.'

'Oh,' I said. I presumed the faux hippy persona my brother cultivated meant he had relaxed into middle age. 'Maybe France changed him,' I said.

'Not at all. You Irish are so uptight; all that soggy guilt you carry around.' Ivy pushed me through the hall of the apartment, which was lush with pot plants. 'This is the salon.'

I wanted to make some retort about the English – Ivy was a Londoner – but the room was lovely and I was jealous; it was like a scene from another age with its long windows that filtered light. I took in the picture rails and the crisp antique furniture. It confirmed what I had always thought: everyone else's home was better than mine. Even my dead brother's.

'What a smashing room,' I said, though I hadn't intended to be pleasant.

'Bernard loved the salon. He used to sit with the windows open, smoking and looking out. It's a pity you never saw him here, Fergus.'

'Smoking?' I said.

Ivy mentioned that my nephew – Nicholas – would be coming to stay while I was there. 'He lives in Lyons now,' she said. 'He's been travelling to Paris once a fortnight since Bernard died. Checking up on me.'

'Nick was so young the last time I saw him. Twelve years old, maybe.'

I didn't say I thought Nicholas was wasted on Bernard, or that my envy of their relationship was one of the things that kept me away. My marriage was never blessed with children.

Since Bernard died I had been dreaming about insects: earwigs in my bath and shitty woodlice on my pillow, that sort of thing. The dreams disturbed my sleep and I had been awake early every day for six weeks. Then the morning chorus would start up. In Ivy's spare bedroom, I dreamt there were moths landing on my face. The birds in Paris were even more vigorous than the ones at home; they whirred on the balcony outside my window, hour after hour. I opened it, flapped my hands and shooed, but they ignored me.

'What are those awful birds?' I asked Ivy at breakfast.

'Sparrows – they go a bit batty at this time of year; they drove Bernard mad.' She poured my tea.

'They're infuriating,' I said. I told her about my dreams: about the creepy-crawlies, the wakefulness, the whole lot. 'The dreams started after I'd heard Bernard was dead. And it's not just insects either. All my dreams are crazy since he died. I dreamt that jam was evil; there were health warnings about it.' I sipped my tea and looked at Ivy; she had a collectedness that I would have liked for myself, her face was always set and calm. I wanted to stop blabbing, but I went on: 'I wouldn't mind only apart from one recurring dream I've been having for years, I don't normally remember anything.'

'Funny, me neither,' Ivy said. 'But I dreamt last night that Bernard was in the chair beside our bed. He never sat there. It felt very real and I wanted him to go away.'

'Oh,' I said. Her dream had trumped mine.

'Are you afraid of burial, Fergus?'

'I don't know. What do you mean?'

'Well, maybe the insects in your dreams have something to do with that,' she said. 'You know, *"The worms crawl in, the worms crawl out; the worms play pinochle on your snout"*,' she chanted. I was baffled. 'It's a song, Fergus.'

'So it appears. Well, I've never heard it.' I drank my tea and examined her; what an odd woman, I thought.

She waved her napkin in my face. 'Oh, cheer up, Fergus. Why don't we go out for a walk? Clear the clouds.'

We took a Métro to the eighth arrondissement and emerged above ground near the Champs. I was familiar enough with Paris not to be enthralled or smothered by it, but I was happy to be there breathing its strange, pure air that endured even in summer. I've always liked that as a city it's both familiar and unknowable: the Eiffel tower pokes like the folly that it is from the quai; the Tour Montparnasse stretches blank and ugly over Saint Germain; the people are singular and entrenched in their lives – almost perfect.

Paris is a city, I've often thought, that can provoke both lust and revolt in the dullest of hearts. I had always been fond of the place and it galled me that my brother made it his own because I had not.

For a small woman, Ivy walked surprisingly fast. We passed café after café where the people inside mouthed to each other across tables like fish in aquariums; they drank coffee and water, ate croissants and omelettes. Smokers cuddled outside under awnings, ignoring one another as they aimed blue jets into the street. Ivy marched on, pointing out shops that, by their scant window displays, seemed to sell nothing at all. She brought me to the place du Carrousel, where the guillotine had fallen on thousands of necks.

'Imagine the blood that flowed here once,' she said, with a kind of manic glee.

'Just imagine,' I said. I was overheated and, because I was wearing my stupidest shoes, my feet hurt.

Ivy waved a hand at the Seine and said she loved the river. 'And the bridges, Fergus. My God, the bridges. The French know how to look after their city – they pour millions into its upkeep. Billions!'

'Can we stop for a cup of tea; something to eat?' I asked meekly, when she seemed determined to walk as far as the Marais without stopping.

'Of course, Fergus. You have to try the croque-monsieur in a place I know off the rue de Rivoli. They do the best ones.'

The bistro we entered had a weird smell – something foreign lurked behind the normal coffee-and-bread scent; it bothered me but I couldn't get to what it was. We took a seat by the window and Ivy chattered in French to the waiter. Two women sat across from us, stroking their lapdogs and talking quietly. Ivy pushed her arms over her head and grunted.

'Ah,' she said, 'that feels good.'

'Will you stay here, now that Bernard is gone?' I asked.

'Where would I go? This is home.'

'I thought you might go back to London.'

'There's nothing for me in England.'

I was glad to be sitting down and I stretched my legs under the small table. Ivy looked as if she might jump up any second; there was a giddiness about her that didn't suit a mourning widow, I thought.

'You miss him, I suppose,' I said.

'Like air,' Ivy answered.

The waiter slipped my croque-monsieur in front of me; I poked approvingly at the gruyère that lapped from the sides of the bread. He set down a pichet of white wine and I poured for both of us. Ivy urged me to eat, saying her dish would take a little while. I attacked the croque with my knife and fork but abandoned them in favour of my hands. It was delicious – the bread high and light, the ham salty. The waiter came towards us again – swerving his tray over the heads of other customers – and served Ivy with a huge fish. Its teeth protruded in gnashing spikes and the gelatinous marble of its eye glared at me. I couldn't believe that I hadn't realised the disconcerting smell in the bistro was the smell of fish.

'I'm an ichthyophobe,' I squeaked, fanning my face with my napkin.

Ivy was already filleting the fish's skin; she lifted her eyes to look at me. 'What did you say, Fergus?'

'I said I am an *ichthyophobe*; I can't let you eat that fish at this table.'

Ivy clattered her cutlery onto her plate. 'And what the hell is an ichthyophobe?'

'I'm allergic to fish, you stupid woman!' I pushed back my chair and hurried from the bistro, gulping in the air on the street as soon as I got outside. I was nearly flattened by a man on roller-blades and immediately I had that why-did-I-leave-my-house distress that I always get when I'm away. I kneaded my eyes with my knuckles.

'First insects, then birds, now fish. What next?' I heard Ivy say. I turned to see her at my side. I was still trying to breathe after the shock of the fish's horrible face and bulging scales; after its stink. Ivy put her hand on my arm. 'Do you want to see Bernard's resting place, Fergus?' she said, and I nodded.

Bernard and I were close as young boys, the way brothers near in age often are; we shared a grudging camaraderie and spent a lot of time in each other's company – hurling, roaming the fields, lighting fires. But we also never missed a chance to puck the head off each other, or rat to our mother about some small crime. We walked to school and tormented cats together; we slept in the same room at night. He was a year older than me and started young into girls – around eleven – so our drift started then.

I thought about Bernard and our wasted friendship as Ivy and I stood in front of the memorial wall in the cemetery; the foxy smell of yew trees filled my nose.

'You cremated him,' I said.

'At his request.'

'God, our mother would have hated this.' I looked around. 'So, his ashes are in there?' I pointed to the wall.

Ivy fidgeted with the strap of her handbag; she lifted her face to the sky and puffed out a breath. I watched her and waited for an answer.

'You know, Fergus, I was going to tell you his ashes were in that wall, but I don't feel right doing it now,' she said. 'You remind me so much of him sometimes it's like you *are* him.' She looked up at me. 'I took him home to the apartment. He's at home.'

'Well, if that was what you wanted,' I said.

Ivy grinned at me, looking a little guilty, and I smiled. I looked back at Bernard's name and dates on the memorial wall. I wanted to feel worse standing there, for my lost brother and for our mother who believed that cremation meant no chance of an afterlife, but I didn't. I couldn't muster any of the sadness that had been dogging me for weeks.

'He's safe from the insects at least,' Ivy said. 'No worms will play pinochle on *his* snout.'

I sniggered and Ivy burst into chuckles; she wriggled the laugh through her whole body and stamped her feet. The two of us fell into tear-spilling convulsions, holding each other up and shaking off spasms of laughter. Some teenagers, who were making a pilgrimage to a rock star's grave, studied us and smiled. One boy did an impression of Ivy's foot-stamping and that made us both hoot loudly.

'We're turning this cemetery into a pantomime,' I said. 'Let's go.'

Ivy linked my arm; we waved to the teenagers and strolled through the graveyard, admiring the plots and the jungle of headstones. Ivy was not really like an English person, I thought, she didn't look at you as if from a great height. She was unpredictable, outspoken – rude, even – but warm. Yes, warm.

Ivy had used Bernard's ashes to fertilise the pot-plants in the apartment's hallway. His empty urn sat in the armoire in the room where I slept. I thought about it each night before putting my head down, after a day spent with Ivy. We walked the places she and Bernard had walked: the Bois and the Jardin du Luxembourg; the open-air food markets and the riverbank. We ate in the bistros they had loved to go to together and we talked and talked.

We sat in her salon in deep sunlight one evening, after hours of walking, and drank wine. Nicholas, my nephew, was due from Lyons but he was late, so we had eaten dinner without him.

'Bernard was mad for girls,' I said, wanting to talk about my brother; I felt we had been neglecting him.

'Oh, always,' Ivy said.

'Was he faithful do you think?'

'What does it matter, Fergus? I loved him.'

'I spied on him with a girl called Caroline Clear once, when we were kids. They were in the woods, against a tree, and he had his hand under her skirt, moving it fast. I could see her knickers and I was shocked because they were navy blue – a little girl's underwear.' I sipped my wine and Ivy looked at me, her expression bemused. 'Caroline became well known in the media and I could never watch her TV show, remembering Bernard's furious groping. It made me hate both of them. He found out I'd been eyeballing and hit me a few digs in the face; I had bruises on my cheeks. There was never a thimbleful of trust between us after that.'

'Such a pity you two didn't stay close,' Ivy said. 'You're so very alike.'

I looked out the window. The starlings were pegged onto the balcony grilles like ornaments, not making a sound; a leaden moon skulked over the rooftops even as the sun went down.

'Will Nicholas make it from Lyons tonight?' I asked.

'It's a bit late now.'

'I'll sleep well,' I said, waving my full wine glass at Ivy.

'No bad dreams for either of us, hopefully.'

I told Ivy my worst dream, the one that nagged at me. 'It's always the same: I've killed someone, an old neighbour from Watergrasshill. Years later his dis-membered body is discovered and I realise I'm about to be exposed as the murderer. It catches me around the neck that dream; I'm so afraid that it's true. That I'm a killer. Thanks be to God I always wake up, but it takes a while to get over it.'

'I hate those ones that linger. That dream is probably about guilt, Fergus. You know, about unfinished business.' She sipped her wine. 'I had a funny one this morning, actually; I've just remembered it. There were two smart-mouthed kids, yapping all this clever stuff at each other. It felt like the kids were me and Bernard. Or me and you.' She frowned.

'I was in your dream?' I said. 'Well, I'm honoured. Mine seem to have dried up – no more spiders, et cetera.'

I liked our small ritual of dream dissection; I enjoyed Ivy's insights and her reports on what she dreamt about. I stretched my arm and clinked my glass off hers. Her face was gilded by the setting sun; she looked radiant – beatific, almost – and it felt natural to lean forward and put my lips to hers. Her mouth was soft, which surprised me, and I kissed deeper, slipping my tongue against Ivy's, testing. She kissed me back and pulled away only to put down her glass. I placed mine beside hers on the coffee table and we fell on each other. Her body yielded under me but the sofa was tiny and we were soon sliding onto the floor.

'Fergus. Bedroom,' Ivy said, her breath clashing off mine and her hands ruffling madly inside my shirt.

We jumped up and went to her and Bernard's room. Ivy pulled her jersey dress over her head in one swift yank. I noticed that her knickers were too big

– they sagged over her belly. I was about to remark on it but I said nothing. Maybe I was growing kinder; maybe Ivy was having an influence.

We leapt into her bed and stared at each other. We made love furiously and I felt like the most able lover in the world; all our movements seemed to glide and meld. Her skin was butter soft, her thrusting strong and rhythmic; I welcomed the velvet pulse of her. I had to hold myself back and I stopped more than once to caress and look at her, to slow myself down. I traced my fingers over her sunburnt skin, over the ivy leaf on her chest. She wrapped her legs around my waist and urged me on. I couldn't believe this was Ivy; I couldn't believe it was me.

Ivy retrieved our wine glasses from the salon. We sat up in her bed, my arm around her shoulder, and drank. Though we were naked, we both acted as if nothing out of the ordinary was happening. I kissed the top of her head.

'You know, you can't be that much of an ichthyophobe,' she said.

'Why's that?'

'I'm a Pisces.'

We both laughed; I pulled her closer to me and fingered her chest.

'Don't get sunburnt again,' I said; 'it's irresponsible. Keep yourself safe.'

'Oh, stop it, you sound like Bernard.'

'Well,' I said.

The bedroom was dim, lit only by the moonlight that scattered across the floor from the window.

I heard the door-handle click before Ivy did. I clenched my body and watched the door open wider and wider.

'Maman?' a voice said. And then, in a higher pitch, 'Papa?' Nicholas stood in the doorway, staring at me, his face confused. 'Papa?' he said again and moved towards us.

'It's me, Nicholas. Uncle Fergus.'

He lunged forward. 'What the fuck?' he shouted.

Nicholas turned and left the room quickly. Ivy climbed from the bed, breasts swinging and wine slopping from her glass onto the eiderdown.

'Nicholas,' she called. 'Nick!' She followed him out to the salon and I slowly got up and pulled on my clothes.

I hung my outfit for the morning on the armoire. It kept me awake half the night, looming like a lurker in the room. I got up and opened the armoire to look for Bernard's urn. It stood on a shelf with his folded T-shirts and jeans: it was a black porcelain pot and it reminded me of a biscuit barrel. I took it out and snapped off the lid; the inside was ashy. I slid one finger over the inner wall of the urn and looked at the white residue it left on my skin.

'Goodbye, Bernard,' I said, and instantly felt maudlin and foolish. I put the urn back.

The next morning Nicholas didn't come out of his room and I woke Ivy to tell her I was leaving.

'Good morning, you,' she said and patted the edge of her bed, so I sat.

'Tell Nicholas I'm sorry,' I said.

'There's no need, Fergus. I'm not sorry. Last night you were my *péché mignon* – one adorable little weakness. I'm allowed that.'

'I upset Nicholas.'

She took my hand and kissed it. 'He'll get over it.'

'Thanks for everything, Ivy. You've helped me.'

'And you me, Fergus,' she said.

We kissed and I agreed I would come back to Paris before Christmas and stay for a fortnight. I left for the airport – half-bereft, half-ecstatic – and made my way home to Watergrasshill.

I never saw Ivy again. That November, in her Paris apartment, she took her own life. She sent me a long, rambling letter but she was already gone by the time I read her words. She said she couldn't go on without Bernard. She missed him far too much; she missed her life as it used to be and, she said, the present was no good to her.

'The past, for me,' she wrote, 'is a picture etched on glass, almost visible but not quite.'

And it was safely in the past that Ivy most wanted to be.

Moongazer

$\mathscr{U}$p they come from the River Corrib like wild arrows: *tharump, tharump, tharump*. I can feel their gut and sinew deep in my breast as they bolt past. They settle then in their shallow beds and I stay as still as granite, except for hitching my shawl this way or that, for comfort. The sky is mackerel and buttermilk. I have to wait.

I pass the time by remembering the island and its clear air; it never stank like this town. And I think of my husband, swallowed up by the sea so many years ago, his young body bloated and salty when I got him back. We were two months wed; we hadn't even made a child.

Dusk closes down over the riverbank by and by. The moon, I see, will be a poor lamp tonight – it is just a paring. I take a snare from my sack and set to work. I tie the snare to the sturdiest branch I can find and secure it with two twigs; I sweep my hand underneath to check it is not too low, not too high. Then I go back to my perch by the river and wait. My bonnet string itches my chin so I tease it with one finger. The grumble from my belly grows loud. I wonder if the hares will cuddle down and not bother to come out at all. But they do.

One by one I hear them lollop about; they stop, testing the air with their noses. One of them – a doe – is a moongazer and she sits on her haunches and turns her face to where the slice of moon rests. Then on she goes.

She is my lady.

I follow her down the narrow run where I set the snare and, sure enough, she is snagged there. The doe lurches forward and gets bogged deeper into the wire hoop.

'Go easy, girl,' I say, rubbing the plush length of her. 'You're a fine lassie.' I grab her ears and flip her; I slice her pale belly in one quick move. Out plops a sack of leverets and I gasp. I look closer: three little ones in all. 'You were luckier than I,' I tell the doe.

Tossing the babies into the long grass, I take their mother to the river to gut and wash her. It takes a while to find the cinders from my last fire but soon I am heating the doe's carcass over the flames. The smell of cooking makes me weak and I pluck strings of pink meat and gobble them back.

Looking into the fire I think again of Seáinín and the hours we spent wrapped around each other in the settle bed – every night of our marriage – with the turf glowing in the grate. I curse God for not letting a baby take inside me; for not leaving me something of my man to hold onto. If only I had a son to mind me, I wouldn't have to scratch around on the banks of the Corrib, killing young mothers to fill my gut. I raise my face to the crescent moon and beg her to forgive me.

Scullion

Sometimes I want to say to her, 'Your man has a better time in a short night with me than he has with you in a long week.' But my mammy always says it is cannier to hold a secret under your tongue and not blurt it out from annoyance. I often feel a glow inside myself because the scutty bitch doesn't know a thing.

I pour the water for her bath and help her in. She is slack and lumpy from having babies – I see her belly rolling under the wet linen. My body sits high where it should and my skin pulls tight over my bones. Her hair is thicker and longer than mine, prettier all in all. I would wash my hair more, if I was let; then it might not look so dull.

'Leave me now,' she says, leaning back into the hot water. 'I will call if I need you.'

I take the pitcher with me to refill it from the stove and, sure enough, I'm not gone three steps down the stairs when she is roaring out.

'Mary! Get back here.'

'God give me patience,' I say, hearing my mammy's voice in my own, a thing that makes me smile. I don't call back that I am coming directly because she thumped me before for shouting. I enter the room.

'Hand me that novel,' she says, and clicks her fingers. I'd love to snap the fingers off her, one by one, when she does that. I fetch the book from the nightstand and hand it to her; I don't need to be told to leave.

She talks about me like I am deaf as a fish. Her and the sister sit, sewing pictorial samplers all day, holy prayers and flowers and God knows what. All sweet and close while they take apart my character and don't bother to put me back together again. That sister of hers is always in the house; you would think she had no home of her own.

'Mary has a temper you see, Jane,' Herself says. 'She is loose-tongued and prone to fits of anger.' She looks over at me, to make sure I am listening, but I pretend that I'm not.

'Our maid-of-all-work is like your Mary – a slattern with a violent nature,' her sister says.

They do the same with everyone they know while I put coals on the fire and serve tea. This one is a prig, they say; that one is too plain to net a husband. After a time, they lose the manners of their upbringing and start cackling and squawking like rooks. All that ends when they hear Himself come in; then they are back to discussing the rain and what meals they have planned for the week and how the health of their children fairs.

Herself's name is Ursula; he calls her 'little bear' and 'peteen'. She's as wide as a bear anyway, that much is true. The three children – all girls – are white-haired like her, but they are pleasant little things. Like their father. They come to the kitchen and I dandle them until Cook scolds me.

'Mary, stop idling,' she says; 'there's plenty of work crying out to be done.'

The children kiss me with their soft, wet mouths. I hug them in turn.

'You are blessed little women,' I say; 'the best in all of Ireland.' I kiss each of them on the forehead. 'Now, get out of my sight.' I run them, laughing, from the kitchen.

'You're making trouble for yourself, girl. Missus won't thank you for molly-coddling those lassies.'

'What do I care what *she* says?'

'Go easy, Mary. The family are separate to us. All of them.'

Cook heaves a tureen of spuds onto the table and tells me to peel and eye them.

Himself comes to me most nights; I know the sound of his stockinged feet in the passageway. He lets himself in and closes the door.

'Mary, are you sleeping?' Always the same question.

'I am not.'

He slips out of his clothes and into my bed. His feet are cold and he tastes, usually, of smoke and his after-dinner port. He kisses me like a madman, slobbering his tongue all over my face and neck in a way that is so welcome to me. It never takes long for the hot hardness of him to push against my leg, then on up into me. Deeper and deeper he climbs inside and rocks up and up until, with a squeak, his chest collapses onto mine and we lie in each other's arms, breathing like two horses after a run. I comb his black hair with both hands and he sleeps a while; I feel the wetness seep under me and I like it.

'Mary, my lamb,' he says, when he wakes. He laughs through his teeth, a little ssss-ing noise that is peculiar to him, and he kisses my nose. Then he leaves.

There are marks on my arms and thighs from all his pushing and squeezing; I examine the bruises in the morning light, delighting in them as if they were jewels. I press on the sore spots during the day to remind myself of him; I poke their softness until the pain is hard to bear and I smile, holding my memories of his body and smell to myself.

Herself and her sister are talking in lowered voices. There is a hush to the whole room and I try to go easy while I rake the fire.

'I have missed my monthly flow,' Herself says.

'For many months, Ursula?'

'Too many.'

I am not a foolish person, but suddenly I know that what they speak of is true for me too; the shock settles over me like a cold cloak. I have been feeling peaked; my blood has not flowed. Something has been growing under my apron for months and I have chosen not to see it. I let the fire-irons fall and they bang off the hearth. The two sisters don't even raise their heads. They begin to speak about babies. Babies-on-the-way and them not being welcome and the like. My stomach lurches into my mouth and I hastily leave the room.

'Mary, are you sleeping?'

'No, Sir.'

He muscles in beside me, sighing. 'I am weary tonight,' he says. His port and tobacco breath is rich; I must speak before his mouth locks over mine and it is too late for chatter. I prop up on one elbow and draw the candle on the sill closer, the better to see his face.

'I am carrying your baby,' I say.

He looks into my eyes and laughs; he thinks I am making fun. 'Don't be foolish, my lamb. You're not old enough to be with child.'

'I have been bleeding since I was ten.'

He stares hard at me. 'Quite the woman at fourteen, then,' he says. 'What will you do?'

'Do, Sir?'

'With the baby, Mary. What will you do with the child?'

His face looks deformed in the flickering candlelight; it frightens me. I snuggle my head under his arm. 'I will send the baby home to my mother,' I say, though I know that no such thing will be possible.

'Well then,' he says, and pushes his hand between my legs.

My lying-in takes place in my room under the eaves on a wet autumn day; Cook attends me. Herself's lying-in takes place in her bedroom, with Doctor Cleary and the midwife. Over the thrumming of rain, I hear her shouts rise and fall, out of step with my own; I hear her husband's voice, loud with sympathy and succour. The rain eases and it is quiet until I hear wailing that is not that of a baby. I labour on, pain banding my belly; I grunt and push and groan. After one long bear down, my son screams air into his lungs and wriggles red and fierce in Cook's arms. She laughs and holds him up. I put him to my breast and Cook stands over me, proud as any husband.

'The bonniest of baby boys,' she says, and then she sits on the bed and weeps into her blood-streaked hands. Like me, she is fagged out.

Cook leaves us for a time. I hold my son and breathe his warm breath as if it were my own. I examine his puffed up eyes, the thin nails on the ends of each finger. Cook comes back with hot tea. She takes the baby, helps me to sit and drink a cup.

'There now, Mary.'

'Thank you, Cook.'

She swaddles my son. 'The Master's baby was born dead,' she says.

'God between us and all harm. Another girl?'

'A boy. The shakings of the Missus's bag he was.'
She lowers her voice. 'Mary, I think you should take
your son and get away from here.'

But I have nowhere to go. My mammy is ashamed
of me and has told me not to come home again.

My son is one day old and I haven't taken my eyes
from him. He is like neither me nor his father; he is
wholly himself. He yawns like a kitten, wide and content; he is quiet, watchful. His dark blue eyes seem to
take in all around him. Cook fusses over me, as taken
with the baby as I am.

'Leave him out of your arms, Mary,' she says,
more than once, 'or you will ruin him.'

But she can scarcely let go when she gets to hold
him and she kisses his soft cheeks and sings to him.
She hands him back to me when he whimpers, knowing who he needs.

Himself comes to my room; it is the first time in
months and the first time ever in daylight. I glance
from Cook to him.

'Hand the boy to me,' he says, in a voice so stern
it makes me jump.

'I'm nursing him; he'll cause bedlam if I give him
to you. Let him drink and rest.'

'Give that child to me, Mary, and we will say no
more about it. You can stay.'

'Stay, Sir? I don't intend to leave.' I shift the
baby to my other breast and Cook tries to cover
me.

The Master lunges and grabs the baby; he pulls my son off my breast and I cry out in pain. The baby yelps in fright.

'Give him back!' I try to climb from the bed and blood rushes between my legs. I flop back, weak. 'Cook, take him,' I shout; 'take him!'

But Cook folds her arms and watches as the Master walks away with my son.

They name him William, after Himself. He is kept in a room beside Herself's with a wet-nurse for company. The nurse is a reedy woman with a face as pink as a piglet and I worry that William is not getting enough milk. I rarely see him and never close by. His sisters have been told not to come to the kitchen anymore. Himself does not come to my room under the eaves anymore either. The wet-nurse eats dinner with us in the kitchen some evenings – when the house has company – but we cannot get her to speak much.

'Is your charge a good baby?' Cook asks, her voice high.

'As good as most,' Nurse says.

'Is he hardy?' I say, though my body aches just in talking about him.

'A greedy baby, I would say.' She twists her gob into a grin and I want to smack her.

'Healthy,' Cook says, with a nod to me that is meant to provide comfort. But what comfort is there when I can't even hold my own son?

In my room, Cook holds cabbage leaves and hot compresses against my breasts; I can barely move with the pain of the engorgement. I weep into Cook's apron and she says 'There, there, Mary; all will be well.' But I know that she is vexed.

She gives an excuse to Herself as to why I can't lift or carry, and sends me out to pick kale and blackberries. I am moving along the bushes near the bottom of the vegetable garden, bending low to pluck the berries, when I see Himself and Herself leave in the carriage. I fill the basket and return to the kitchen.

'They're gone somewhere,' I say to Cook.

'To Dublin. They won't be dining here for the rest of the week,' she says. 'It's ourselves and the children. And the nurse.'

Cook looks at me for a long moment and I try to gather what her eyes are saying, but she moves away and pours water onto the kale to wash it. I stand, stuck to the floor like a clump of muck, until Cook looks over at me again. She tosses her head upwards, widening her eyes, and I leave the kitchen for the back stairs.

Baby William is all alone in the nursery. I lift him from his cradle and hold him to me; the sweet smell of his scalp makes me giddy. His small body is sturdy I am glad to find; I move my lips across the fur of his hair and hold him close and closer.

'Baby, baby,' I say, and rock him in my arms. 'Baby, it's your mammy.'

I sit in the chair and lift my breast to his mouth. He takes the nipple and sucks, making small, happy mewls; it hurts but I can hear the hot milk fill his throat and that, not the pain, makes me cry. I lift him onto the other breast. He opens his eyes, then rolls them back; he looks ossified and content. He is so warm, so clean, so new; my son.

'A changeling. That's what they call the child that replaces the *real* baby.'

Nurse has crept in like a pooka and she stands over me.

'William is no changeling; he's my son.'

'He's your Master's son.' She extends her arms to take William; her peculiar black hair is severe; I am afraid of her. 'Give him to me.'

I slip my smallest finger into William's mouth and his tongue sucks backward off my breast. 'There now,' I say and rub his soft cheek off my own and hand him to Nurse.

She bundles him under one arm and slaps my head with her free hand. 'Do not enter this room again.'

'Mary, are you sleeping?'

The words confuse me because they don't match the voice. 'I'm... it's...' I sit up in my bed.

'Mary, we have to act now.' Cook holds her candle near her face so that I can see her. She tells me to get dressed and gather my things. 'Nurse is passed out in the kitchen – I gave her a dose of port.' Cook cackles and then slaps her hand over her mouth. 'Stay here and get ready,' she whispers.

I stuff my change of clothes and my hair combs into a pillow slip; I wrap the leather purse my mammy gave me in my clean under-things for safety. I put on my bonnet and shawl and wait. Cook comes quietly through the door with the baby. She kisses his face over and over, then places him in my arms.

'Change his name, Mary,' she says and pushes a wad of money at me, which must surely be all she has.

'No, I can't, Cook,' I say, trying to shove it back but she shakes her head.

'Take it, child; take it. There are boats to the New World from Queenstown. Maybe you'll go on one and be safely away.' I grip her hand and both of us weep. 'Godspeed, Mary.'

I gather my bundles tightly to me – my possessions and my son – and leave.

Easter Snow

*T*he cold in Manhattan is a cold I have never felt before. Wind shoots up the slits of the avenues and settles over everything like a shroud. Then it snows and the umbrella man on our corner changes his sing-song from 'It's a-raining a-cats and a-dogs' to 'It's a-snowing like a-Christmas'.

'You have single-handedly made this man rich,' Thomas says, but buys me another umbrella anyway – a candystriper – and I promise not to lose it.

The umbrella man grins and says, 'It's a-snowing like a-Christmas, lady, hah?'

'It is,' I say.

Thomas looks like the Child of Prague. He has that same prissy superiority and baby-blond hair but, in a way, this is what I like best about him. His sweet looks make up for other things. Lacks.

We battle down Eighth Avenue, tucked under the umbrella, and are assailed by a crowd that rush up from the subway, like people fleeing a war zone.

'Jesus H. Christ,' Thomas says, stumbling to get out of a man's way. 'Watch it, buddy.'

I cling to his arm and we push on. I watch my boots disappear into the snow with each step and listen to the chug-and-sump they make, audible even over car horns and sirens. The snow muffles the city's usual clamour and I welcome that. I am from a quieter place – a country of villages, where the odd tractor makes the biggest noise, and the buildings do not try to suck the breath out of the sky.

Thomas claims not to believe that my home place has seven pubs, but only one church and one shop. 'I know you guys can drink, but *seven* pubs. Why?'

I answer this with a shrug; he requires nothing else.

The snow dazzles my eyes though it makes the air dark; it drifts and squats. Snowploughs plod up and down the island, shoving snow along in small, ineffectual loads. I could stride easier if Thomas would let me go but he wants to keep me close so, wrapped together under the umbrella, we perform a shuffle and dodge down the avenue. His arm around me is stifling; I am like a nestling trapped under its mother's wing. I pull away from him and walk a little ahead, letting snowflakes melt in my hair. Thomas shakes the snow-coating off the umbrella.

I reach the corner of 35th Street and stop to watch an SUV skirl in a magnificent arc on the roadway. Passersby cry out, but I am mesmerised by the beauty of the skating car and I stand and gawp, even when its bumper is nearly upon me. Thomas leaps and pushes me into a snow bank; the car clips his leg. He winces and curses. There is a gash and blood but he says, 'I'm OK, I'm OK.'

The waiting room is warm and empty. Thomas parks me next to the radiator and I place my gloved hands on it and watch vapours rise. He checks the tear in his jeans and wads tissues against the cut. A nurse hands him a bandage; she stands over him and tut-tuts.

'Goddamn snow,' she says. 'What is this weather about? I got chocolate bunnies in my bag!'

My name is called and we enter the room. I lie on the table and the doctor takes her wand from its cradle; she smiles at me and asks if I'm ready. Thomas holds my hand and we turn together to face the screen. Our child is there, a pulsing egg; he sends out his slow, sonic whirr to us through the blizzard that surrounds him. We hear it and catch it and take it home with us through the snow.

Spelunker

A dog called Robot discovered the cave paintings at Lascaux; Robot who belonged to a boy named Marcel. The dog was chasing a hare and when he disappeared down a hole, Marcel and his friends followed. What treasure to stumble upon; it must have been like unearthing the first truffle and finding it tasted of heaven. I have often imagined how they must have felt when their bicycle lamps glanced across all those deer and bulls and Lowryesque men; the galloping horses. My mother loved horses; she was as natural around them as I am unnatural.

These are the things occupying my mind as the aeroplane lifts over the Irish Sea and heads south towards France. I'm not really thinking about Robot, of course, or Marcel and his friends – they glide under my thoughts – but of my mother and the things she

loved. Horses; my sister and me; her home in county
Dublin; and, despite everything, my father.

I sleep on the bus from Beauvais to Porte Maillot,
waking only as it pulls into the car park under the
shadow of the Concorde La Fayette. Paris smells of
rain and it carries itself with its peculiar hectic leisure
as always: car horns parp, workers stroll with purpose
and women dander with toy dogs. The streets are
having their morning clean and water rushes by the
footpath carrying sweet wrappers, leaves and a lone
baby shoe.

I walk down to the Champs to meet Mado outside
the Citroën showroom, as arranged. We kiss, three
times to each cheek. Mado is not anyone I know; she
was put on to me by a friend of an acquaintance. She
is small and neat and has the weary confidence that
I always associate with the French. After coffee in a
bistro and some brief instructions, she sways opposite me on the Métro and I wait for her signal. We
change to line two and pass through Place de Clichy
and Pigalle. As we approach Barbès Rochechouart,
she nods; we both move towards the doors and get
off the train as soon as it stops. I follow her to the
end of the platform and pretend to study the Métro
map; Mado sits on a bench and speaks into her mobile
phone.

The station clears and Mado moves, slipping off
the end of the platform and into the tunnel. When
I slide up behind her, she takes my hand and pulls
me though a doorway; her fingers are taut on mine.
We are now in The Rat Hole and it leads to The

Undercut, a train station that has never been open to the public and never will be. We flick on our torches and, hand-in-hand, slowly make our way across the rough floor, climbing over sleepers and piles of cement. It is warm and getting warmer. I hear music and voices echoing towards us. We come to a slack hillock of stones; a dull sunrise spills above it. We climb up and stop at the top of the slope; Mado lets go of my hand.

'We're here,' she calls, waving her torch into the cavern of the ghostspace before us.

Heat blasts me and I'm glad of my T-shirt and light trousers; the smells are of oil and something stagnant like old water. My eyes adjust to the dim light and The Undercut comes into focus: there is no track laid where the train would have travelled, but there are opposing platforms and acres of cement wall, most of it already alive with colour. I feel saliva juicing my tongue. We run down the stony hill and stand at the bottom.

A man steps from the shadows. 'Bienvenue, Mr D. I am Renard,' he says, and shakes my hand. In our world, real names are not shared.

'Good to meet you, Renard,' I say.

'You will work there,' he says, pointing to the opposite platform, where most of the curved wall is free. Further along I can make out the figures of other artists, stepping back to appraise what they have done and adding touches.

I toss my backpack into the track-space and jump after it; I clamber onto the far platform where lights are set up on tripods to help me see my wall. As I turn, I see Renard and Mado kiss deeply, his hands in her hair. I open my pack and take out my cans, mask, gloves and stencils.

I have to work fast; this is the last day that The Undercut will ever be open. Shortly, Mado will guide a photographer down here to prove that it all happened, then we will leave and this secret gallery will be sealed. I stand in the semi-dark on the platform, hearing the Métro blasting by above my head, and get ready to work.

Last night, in Dublin, we waked my mother. My auntie laid her out in her bed; she put my mother's maroon dress on her and a slick of lipstick; she curled her hair, broke the curls with her fingers and sprayed them. We stood around the bed and the familiar words of childhood prayers reformed themselves with ease on my lips: *Hail Mary full of grace, the Lord is with thee.* My sister leaned on my arm and cried; candles made the room stuffy and eerie, but also beautiful. My mother held a sprig of lilac in her still hands – her favourite, even though it was the death flower, the bringer of bad luck.

I know my sister will be bewildered by the note I left her but The Undercut is years in the planning and I couldn't let Mado or Renard down. My sister will go to the funeral, sit in the pew and wonder why I have left her to get through such a day on her own. Our father will probably turn up and she will have that to deal with too.

Still, I am not ashamed. My piece here will be a homage to my mother; a shout to her from this dim cave to whatever place of light she occupies now.

I have craved a solitary life since the day I was born. I muddled through school, batting away potential friends. I was the type of child who felt like I was being beaten up, even when I wasn't. Just walking past a gang of kids did that to me – groups and crowds were not places I could ever be. My mother worried about me; I was too much alone, she said, and did her best to provide comfort.

'You'll find a friend who matches who you are,' she would say; 'maybe even a girlfriend.'

It was an incantation to soothe herself. Her tinny hope was too much sometimes but knowing she was there in the background was enough for me. I didn't need the company of others.

'What are we going to do with you, Danny?' she also used to say, and I had no answer.

It is to Lascaux's horses that I now turn for guidance; the horses who would still be galloping silently in the dark if it were not for Robot the dog. I slide on my gloves, tamping between the fingers to tighten them. I flex my hands, pick a can of dun paint and shake it; I spritz the air with it to make sure the nozzle is not clogged. Its smell hangs, rich as new lilac, and I breathe on it. I pull my mask down from my forehead and fix it over my mouth and nose. I spray the curve of a horse's back onto the canvas of the wall and I am off.

A horse fell on my mother when she was a girl and that was when she realised she loved them. She came out of being trapped under the horse with nothing more than muck on her hair and clothes. We loved to hear her tell this story, my sister and I.

'Up I jumped on the horse's back,' she'd say; 'I loved the feel of his oily coat under my bare legs. It was on our neighbour's farm and I was not meant to ride alone. I hugged the horse's sides with my thighs and started to steer him toward the woods, where I wouldn't be seen. Next thing, a car backfired in the yard and the horse reared up; I fell off and the horse came down on top of me, his back to my front. Well, I was so shocked I could say nothing!' This made us laugh because our mother was never short of words. 'By whatever miracle I landed in mud and the horse's weight just pushed me further down into it.' The horse got to its feet and nuzzled her, checking if she was all right. She grabbed his mane and righted herself by hanging on. 'And I laughed then like I'd never laughed in my life. The horse just stood and stared.'

This is what my cave painting will be: the mud-soaked girl; the bewildered horse. I get lost in the building of the scene; my arm moves with the paint can as quickly as my eye roves the wall, mapping the picture. A scribbled spurt of white shows my mother's laughter; the horse is something like a Lascaux animal, something like the silhouette on a Greek urn.

I hear a whistle, and another, but it takes a third blast for me to register it. I turn to see Mado on the opposite platform, two fingers in her mouth. She whistles again, smiles hugely and beckons to me. I toss down my gloves and mask and go to her.

'Two more hours,' Mado says. 'Come and have coffee with us.'

She links me along the platform to where the others have gathered; I shake hands with each of them. We sit, mostly in silence, sipping our coffee and eating brioche. Every so often one of the others glances towards their workspace – planning, probably, their next move, or the finishing one. I close my eyes and horses canter across my sightline; I see my mother, not as a girl but as I knew her, the sturdy woman who laughed through everything. I hear her laughter like a song in my ear. Something cracks in my chest and I feel tears magnify my eyes; I scramble to my feet and start to walk away.

'Mr D,' Mado says. 'I will take you to your hotel once the photographer is finished.'

I turn and nod my thanks to her.

My mother seemed to come alive in the last two weeks.

'I feel giddy,' she said. 'I'm fizzy; it's like my blood is popping instead of flowing.' This made her laugh though it hurt her to laugh. She said she could hear trucks passing on the avenue, all day and all night. 'Are they the horseboxes?' she asked, and then grunted to dismiss the question. 'No, they couldn't be, I suppose.'

Her room smelled pissy like basil leaves but we couldn't open the windows in case she got chilly. It sounds mad but she had a glow around her at the end, my mother; a halo of brightness. She had shrunk and aged but she still had beauty scattered over her: the bountiful eyelashes remained, dipped hammocks of black, and her smile was as charming as ever. My sister and I took it in turns to sit with her so that the other could go out onto the landing and cry.

When my mother was pregnant with me, my father fell in love with someone else. It took him another year to leave and my mother couldn't warm to me, her baby, because I stank of my father's betrayal. But once he left, she said, normal feelings returned. She devoted herself to my sister and me. My father is a blustery joker – idiotic at times – but somehow my mother loved him until the end.

'He's a man who needs coaxing,' she often said and at the time of his affair, she didn't think she could coax enough for him to stay. She didn't have the energy.

I always thought it was odd that my mother fell for him so fully – he was not her equal and she had been locked into the marriage in the first place by becoming pregnant with my sister. Her mother colluded in trapping her because, as my mother said, back then you didn't just do what you wanted to do, you did what everyone else wanted. So, in her own mothering, she gifted us freedom, and we took it.

There are baby handprints on the walls in Lascaux. The painted figures are hunters but the real hands, outlined in red ochre, are from women and children, as well as men. Whole families went down into the caves together to celebrate their lives through art. I spray the last highlights onto my horse and girl and think of those people, of their unity under that glistening limestone.

Mado comes to look at my finished piece. 'It is very haunting,' she says.

I take her hand and slip on a glove; she looks up at me and says nothing. I press her palm to the wall and spray around it. I put my own gloved hand above Mado's and do the same.

'Now we've both signed it,' I say.

'The photographer is here,' she answers.

My hotel is on boulevard de Magenta; I could easily find it myself but Mado insists she will come with me. We walk past a *boulangerie* and its waft makes me realise I am hungry but I don't go in. There is a sweet tension between Mado and me, and I have a feeling some delicate equilibrium is about to be toppled. Mado slips her arm through mine and looks up at me; she places her head on my shoulder. I stop, lean down and kiss her lips. She smiles and we walk on.

Mado checks me into my hotel and comes up in the tiny lift to my room. The bedroom is small but it has big windows that lead onto a balcony. Mado opens them and gets tangled in the voile curtains.

'Ai, ai,' she complains, and I pull the curtains off her and hold her to me. 'You cried,' she says, 'in The Undercut.'

'Yes.' I let her go and sit on the bed.

'Is it something you wish to talk about?'

'Not now.'

Mado nods and starts to unbutton her jeans. Off comes her jacket and her T-shirt; she steps out of her underwear and unhooks her bra. Her clothes lie around her feet and she stands in front of the billowing curtains and looks at me. A streak of light, blue as a moonbeam, illuminates her skin; the traffic on the boulevard sends its cacophony up to the room.

I stand, undress and we lie on the bed. Mado straddles me and pins down my arms. Sweat sparkles like mica on her brow as she moves over me and I pull my arms down and hold her by the waist, stunned that this is happening, and to me. She makes soft mewling noises then plunges forward to kiss my mouth. The room is dark suddenly and we lie together, limbs hooked through limbs.

'I might stay,' I tell her, 'in Paris.'

'I am glad,' Mado says, and she laughs.

Her laughter lifts over the bed and into the air in the room, lustrous and golden. She laughs easily, the way my mother always did, and I know that this is the start of something, the inevitable rise from the dark to the light. I close my eyes and welcome it.

By Ballytrasna

This is where I live now; my travelling has brought me here and it is good enough. My daughter-in-law tries – forcefully some days, gently others – to move me up to the spare bedroom in the cottage, but right here does me fine. It is only a shed but it is cosy like a gypsy caravan I owned once; it smells of clay and insects and the windows are cobwebbed. There is the smell of oil paint, turpentine and linseed too, and clean east Atlantic air hovers over everything.

I enjoy community – the buzz and thrash of family and neighbourhood life – but solitary space suits me the most. Here in my shed I am free to dream, to paint and to unguard my face and body. Today I am painting an apology to my son. Last week I made one comment too many about my lack of grandchildren.

'Do you want to know why you have no grand-kids, Mam?' John said. 'Do you *really* want to know?' He paced around my shed, making dust dance in light beams. 'Maggie and I are incompatible. That's what the doctors say: "incompatible". It's a disaster. So *stop* asking me about it.'

'You could have told me before,' I said; 'talked to me.'

'For what? So you could quiz me about it at every step?' John raked one hand through his hair. 'You haven't a clue, Mam; you don't know what we've been going through.'

I could have contradicted him on that but he started to cry, so for the first time in twenty years I took my son in my arms and rocked him.

Now I am saying sorry to him in the best way I can. I am doing a painting of an orchid for John.

'The flower must express the life lived,' my old teacher always said.

The life lived. I have lived my life in ten different ways and I am still not sure if I've found the best way; the way to make me say 'Yes, *this* is it.'

Earlier today I went to the florist in Ballytrasna and explored the dark cave of the shop until the right orchid for my painting presented itself. I found one with olive green stains that leaked onto white petals and it was perfect.

My painting doesn't look like any work I've done before; the orchid is surreal with a tall building for a stamen and oceanic petals. I use my oil pastels, paletting them on like butter, building up layers of texture that make the orchid and the building and the watery petals come alive. Then I take up my brush to add finer strokes.

John is not my husband's son and he doesn't know this. I have never found a way to tell him. The painting will say it but he won't understand that. The stamen-building represents the place he was conceived in Dublin – a tall seaside hotel. I had gifted myself a trip to the galleries in that city and came home with more than I went there with. It is a lifetime ago. A life-lived ago.

I am cursed with an unChristian figure – men have ogled me since I was twelve. That they still do gives me a silly satisfaction. John's father, though, was not an ogler; he was too self-possessed a man for that. He had the artist's temperament; he was the sort of man who loved women – appreciated all about them – but would never give himself to just one. Not out of malice but because of a gentleness in his loving that left him helpless when someone new came along. I know that makes him sound like any ordinary womaniser but, really, he was a decent man. John resembles him in that.

We met in the National Gallery and our affair drifted over listless years. I don't think my husband knew about my affair but, in the end, I finished it. My marriage was satisfying and John's father didn't try to sweep me out of it, so I stayed. My husband brought John up as ours; I'll never know if he knew. About any of it.

A daytime moon like a circular cloud hangs over the cottage; I step back from my easel, right up to the window to look at it and I see my daughter-in-law in the garden. Her head is tilted to the sky and I leave my shed and the orchid painting to go to her. We both stand, looking up.

'Beautiful, isn't it?' I say. She turns to me and I'm shocked to see a bruise under her eye. My hand flies to touch it. 'Maggie?' I say.

'It's not what you think, Verona.'

'What do I think?'

'That John hit me,' she says.

'Did he?'

Maggie looks away, back up at the moon. 'It *is* beautiful,' she says. She sighs. 'Verona, John and I have decided to go our separate ways. For a while. Just to see.'

Like an opal that holds too much water, my heart cracks; pain pushes through my chest, against my lungs, and I want more than anything to be alone to cry.

'I'm so sorry, Maggie. So sorry.'

She takes my hand and squeezes it and walks back towards the cottage.

The painting is growing properly – it gathers itself to itself almost, it seems, without my help. I stand and add colours but I am at a remove. The picture is luminous: milky whites blend with greens, blues and greys; the whole effect of it pleases me, a feeling I am not used to. The hotel near Dublin Bay, where I made love to a man I was not married to, looks just like I remember it: a glassy beacon reaching for the sky.

The orchid's water petals are vibrant. As my brush dips to the palette then finds the canvas, my thoughts coast from John's father to my husband. He too was a good and decent man.

My husband and I tried for many years to have a baby; when John came he was a miracle. My husband welcomed this wonder-child with different knowledge to mine, but we shared a great love for him. Our son. The baby we thought we could never have.

I was wrong to deceive my husband; the guilt of keeping my secret is the thing that has warped my life's path and made me a drifter, I am sure of it. My life lived. My life half-lived. I am always stopping and starting, forever veering and moving on. I think I should tell John, tell him properly, straight to his face. Maybe it would clarify things for him and Maggie.

John comes down to my shed; he has his overcoat on and a backpack in his hand.

'You're leaving,' I say.

'I have to, Mam. Only for a while. Maggie and I are making each other sad.'

'I made this for you.' I toss one hand towards the easel where the painting sits.

John looks at it for a moment and smiles. 'It's lovely,' he says. 'Keep it for me, Mam.'

'Look at it properly, John. Please. Look into it. There's a message for you there.'

John walks across the floor of the shed and squints at the picture. 'It's unusual. Different to your normal style; the orchid is beautiful. I like it. Yes, I like it a lot.'

'Do you understand it, John?' I say, feeling half-frantic that I might tell him the truth, even worse because I know I can't. Or won't.

'My train leaves in ten minutes; I have to go.' He lunges forward and hugs me.

'I'm sorry, son,' I say. 'He was a good man, your father. A great man.'

'I know that, Mam,' John says. 'Mind the painting for me, I'll be back soon.'

I watch him leave, his father's long stride taking him across the garden, under the cloud-moon, down towards Ballytrasna and the train station that sits beside the east Atlantic sea. I send my blessings after him and place my secret back inside myself, where it belongs.

My Name is William Clongallen

My name is Guillermo Dante and the woman who I called Mama did not give birth to me. It wasn't until my papa died that Mama told me who I was. I knew I looked different – my brothers couldn't let me forget; in a family of dark-skinned boys, I alone was pale-eyed and fair. Mama used to say it was because I was sickly but I never felt anything but robust. She kept me home with her to do my lessons, though I longed to join the others at the Good Shepherd School on Brown Street. My brothers called me *mimao* – mama's boy – until she whacked at their backsides with her broom and they ran screeching. All of Brooklyn belonged to my brothers while I, it seemed, belonged only to Mama.

I was twelve years old when Mama took me to Alejandro's Café to tell me about my mother. Alejandro came out from the kitchen to sympathise with us over papa.

'He was a good man, Selena; a great man.'

'*Muchas gracias*, Alejandro,' Mama said and patted his hand. Alejandro shook and he swiped at tears; it was as if he was the one with a dead husband. Mama thanked him again and ordered coffee for herself and ice cream for me. Alejandro shuffled away.

'Guillermo,' Mama said to me; 'there is something you should know. It is a sad story but you must not cry.'

'I won't cry, Mama,' I said, though I wasn't sure whether I would or not. I had cried over papa but not too much; I was never a favourite of his, like Primo, my eldest brother.

A waiter came over and served Mama's coffee and my ice cream.

'Do you remember Papa told you that he made a great sea trip when you were a baby?'

'He sailed from New York to Spain and then all the way back to New York again.'

'That's right. Well, that ship that papa sailed on stopped at an island called Ireland on its voyage back.'

Mama's face was serious and I didn't like it; I suckled ice cream off my spoon and eyed her.

'Ireland?' I said.

'Yes. And there the boat picked up many people including a poor young woman and her baby boy. Papa, being a kind man, saw that the woman was having troubles so he helped her and the baby, but she was very, very ill and she died on board. Her name was Mary Carter.'

'Mary Carter,' I repeated, wondering if I was supposed to cry because the woman was dead. 'Did we know Mary Carter, Mama? Was she one of us?'

'You knew her, Guillermo, and she knew you.' Mama leaned forward and gripped my fingers. 'She was your real mama, *mi amor*.' Then she began to sob and Alejandro came over and put his hand on her shoulder. Everyone in the café stared while pretending not to. I looked at the lid of Mama's coffee pot which, because it didn't close properly, seemed to smile at me.

Mama waved Alejandro away and continued to speak. 'Mary Carter was buried at sea. Papa took charge of her baby – you – and changed your name from William to Guillermo. He carried you home to me in Brooklyn. Papa brought nothing of Mary's; he did not even take the blanket you were wrapped in.'

Mama shook her head and went on to say that Papa told her all he knew about my mother: that she was from the County of Limerick in Ireland and she had lived in a house called Clongallen with the Cookes. That was all. He forbade Mama to tell me about myself, but she wanted me to know and she took her chance as soon as Papa was cooling in his grave.

*

Before we married, I told Rosita about Mary Carter. I wanted her to know that I wasn't who I appeared to be, though, as I explained to her, I felt fully like myself.

'You must go to Ireland, *mi amor*, and see where you are from,' she said, excited; 'see who your mother was.'

'I'm from Brooklyn, Rosita, and Mama was all the mother I needed.'

'Guillermo, you are Irish by birth. That means something.'

'I am American,' I said, ending the matter.

But the same conversation was repeated over the years as we reared our family of girls; it was always Rosita who started it, with a shy, angry look that meant I was being reproached. I tamped down any gnawing thoughts of Mary Carter, and, to my wife, proclaimed her irrelevant. It wasn't until our eldest daughter had a baby boy, and I saw his helpless, beautiful form, that I felt the need to find out about my birthplace.

I held my grandson up to my wife and said, 'Now I am ready. Now I will go.'

Rosita was afraid of aeroplanes, so I flew alone to Ireland in search of Mary Carter's life. It was a cheerless country. Brooklyn has its share of rain, cold and dark but Ireland was swamped in drizzle and drear from the moment I arrived to the moment I left. I wondered how the people could stand it and I could see why Mary had taken a way out.

I landed at Shannon Airport and within minutes was driving alongside green fields dotted with cows and sheep, their muzzles fixed to the grass in an eternity of grazing. The rain sluiced onto the car and I drove, hunched over the steering wheel, alert to road signs, afraid I would lose my way. I cursed Rosita for making me come to this place; I cursed Mary Carter for being Irish; I cursed the rain.

I spent the night in a guesthouse called Emerald Sunrise; I lay rigid in the bed and slept in half-hour snatches. In the morning, the bleak-faced landlord gave me directions and stood at the door to watch me drive away as if I were the last guest he might ever take in.

Clongallen House looked derelict. It sat high above the surrounding countryside, at the end of an unmade road; its walls were streaked and the windows were shuttered. The grounds were a tangle of bushes and weeds. I parked the car and stood in front of the house: it had been a grand place once, I thought. I walked around the back and saw a light. I knocked at the window and an old woman looked out; I waved, feeling foolish. She unlatched the door.

'Yes?' she said.

'Hullo! My name is Guillermo Dante and I am looking for the man of the house. A Mr Cooke?'

'There's no one by that name here,' she said, and started to close the door.

'I've come all the way from Brooklyn, New York,' I said, stepping forward.

The old woman looked at me. 'Well, you're at the wrong place, Sir.'

I wanted to keep her talking. 'It's a gloomy day, Ma'am,' I said, sticking my hand out to catch the rain.

'Maybe you brought your own gloom,' she said and shut the door.

I stood for a few moments then got back into the car and drove down the overgrown avenue to the small road that lead up to the gates. I travelled for a mile or so and stopped at a pub called Harty's – its lights looked warm through the misty rain. There were a few elderly men at the bar; I took a low seat under a glass box that housed a plump pheasant perched on dead grass.

The barmaid shouted over, 'What will you have?' I looked at the men who were drinking and pointed. 'A bottle of stout,' the barmaid said.

The telephone rang as the barmaid put the glass and bottle in front of me, cutting short whatever she was about to say. She was soon back.

'It's for you,' she said.

I looked up at her. 'What's for me, Ma'am?'

'The 'phone,' she said, as if I were half mad.

I was sure she was mistaken but I got up anyway and followed her into a back kitchen which smelled sour, like cabbage water. I lifted the receiver.

'Hullo?'

'Come up tomorrow,' said a voice.

'I beg your pardon?'

'Come up to Clongallen in the morning and we'll talk.' It was the old woman from the house.

'How did you know I'd be here?' I said.

'Sure where else would you be?' she said and hung up.

I drove back to the Emerald Sunrise and the land-lord acted as if he had never met me before; I stayed in the room I had been in the previous night and, this time, I slept well.

'What business have you here?' the old woman said, accepting the bunch of roses I handed her and tossing them onto a chair. I had driven to the city and back to buy them. She pointed to a fireside couch and I sat down.

'I understand my birth mother lived here once,' I said. 'My name is Guillermo Dante but I was christened William. My mother was called Mary Carter. Or Cooke, I'm not sure.'

She studied me. 'There was no one called Cooke here, I told you that. You'll have tea.' She filled a black kettle at a deep sink.

'And your own name, Ma'am?'

'Never mind my name. I was the cook for the family here. There's hardly a one of them left. What remains are beyond in England.'

'Did you happen to know Mary Carter?'

'I knew her. She was a bold girl and a good girl all in the one sack. She broke her own mother's heart.'

The kettle grunted on the hob and the woman threw some biscuits onto a plate. She sat on a kitchen chair in front of me and folded her hands in her lap.

'Did she break her mother's heart by leaving for the United States?'

She leaned forward. 'By opening her legs to a man who'd never marry her.'

The woman got up suddenly and made tea, stirring the pot lavishly before placing it where the kettle had been. I felt embarrassed, for myself and for her. I wasn't thirsty but I would drink the tea as she had made it. She rose again, poured and handed me a cup.

'Thank you,' I said and took a sip. The woman stood over me, watching.

'Follow me,' she said.

I looked at the teacup in my hand but she was already unlatching a door on the other side of the room, so I left it down and went after her up a freezing staircase. Up and up we went, drawing the mildewed air into our lungs; the cold was cloying, it felt like hands pulling at my face. She stopped at a door in a corridor and I stood beside her, breathing raggedly after the long ascent. Opening the door, she gestured for me to go in. I dipped under the lintel and stood in a tiny, empty room with a low roof.

'You were born in this room,' the woman said.

I whipped around and stared at her. She nodded. I surveyed the dim space; the floorboards were grey and runnels of water had made one wall green. I could hear rain thrashing down on the roof.

'This is the attic,' I said.

'Mary Carter was a servant in this house. Our master, Lord Clongallen, took advantage of her and... well, I delivered you myself.' She squeezed my arm.

'Mary died on the boat crossing to New York.'

The woman gasped and blessed herself. 'No!' she said. 'God be good to her.'

She bent her head and let a low groan, so I held her elbow and we made our way back down the stairs. Our tea had cooled but I put a cup into her hands and she drank. Tears dropped from her eyes and she pushed them away with her sleeve.

'I wondered why I never heard from Mary. I thought she might write; one letter even, to let me know she was safe. God help me, I'm responsible for her death.'

'I doubt it, Ma'am. How could that be?'

'I encouraged her to go. I gave her the fare.'

'You couldn't have known she would take ill,' I said.

'The master and his missus were going to keep Baby William – you – for their own; it wasn't right. You were Mary's child, first and forever.'

'Yes,' I said.

'I should have seen her right. The peteen,' the old woman said. She told me the little she knew about Mary – that she was fourteen years old; that she came from Pallaskenry, a village west of the city of Limerick. She said I looked like Mary but I wasn't sure if she meant it.

'Oh, sure you're the spit of her. I knew it last night.'

'Was she a nice person?' I said. 'You mentioned she was "bold".'

'Mary Carter was lively and had her own mind. She loved children, she certainly did.' The woman smiled. 'Mary was a brazen strap, if you really want to know.'

'Geez,' I said and laughed.

'You have sisters, three of them. The master's girls. They all live in Suffolk in England, they don't come here.'

I nodded and thought about that; I couldn't see how meeting them would improve anything about me or my life. I rose from the chair and offered her my hand.

'Will you tell me your name now?' I said.

She shook her head. 'No. But I can tell you yours: your name is Lord William Clongallen.' She hugged me suddenly. 'God speed, William,' she said, walking me to the door.

I stood outside in the mizzle that drenched the countryside; I stretched my arms over my head and shouted to the sky, 'My name is William Clongallen.' I took a deep breath. 'My name is William Clongallen,' I roared.

A pigeon broke from a tree and futtered skywards before landing on a higher branch. I got into the car and sat for a few moments, staring at the land, the rain, the slate sky; I longed to be home in Brooklyn. The journey before me looked endless. I rested my forehead on the steering wheel then sat up straight.

'My name is Guillermo Dante,' I said and started the engine and drove away.

From Jesus to the Moon

The hotel on Via Palestro was perfect, despite the cinema opposite that offered films with *Girls, Girls, Girls*; that sort of thing has always made me feel empty in the throat. My room had a view of a different street: I overlooked Trattoria Coriolano and a twenty-four hour *farmacia*, which made me feel safe.

I had walked from Termini Station to the hotel, trundling my trolley-case past homeless men with stumps for legs; past the tat market on Via Montebello which also sold fat, sunbursting clementines; and past the basilica with the giant golden statue of Jesus on its roof. That was the church where Eddie and I knelt as newlyweds, hands clasped, and prayed for a long, happy marriage. Well, that is what I prayed for; who knew what Eddie wanted?

Leaning out the window, I studied the length of Via Cernaia, listening to tootling car horns and dance music that exploded from a room below mine. I stretched my face upwards to catch the afternoon sun. I was there to shake off Eddie; I wanted to reclaim Rome. It had been my idea to marry in the Holy City – a girlhood dream – and I didn't want soggy memories to ruin it forever. Even though I guessed that for me there would always be two Romes: the one of my early marriage and the one of my early divorce. It was the latter one that was going to define the place for me; I was determined. I just had to get out into the city, unpeel Eddie from each place that held our ghost selves, and toss him away.

I lifted my handbag and slung it across my body, like I always told Martha to do when she went out on the town with her friends.

'I know, Mam, I know,' she would say, exasperated with me as always, but doing what I asked anyway.

I slipped across the road to the trattoria and ordered tiramisu and a glass of Chianti. I was weary after the flight from Dublin and giddy too. Nothing would be as it was: I would drink at all hours of the day; I would not watch my figure; I would wander the byways and markets; I would be *me*. The tiramisu had a sweet yellow topping and a dose of Marsala underneath; it picked me up like two arms dragging me off the ground. I knocked back the Chianti and wondered if I was in danger of becoming like Eddie; I squashed down the thought. Fuck Eddie. I giggled and the waiter grinned at me, while preening his grey moustache.

On Piazza del Quirinale, I watched all life scatter by: policemen and soldiers, buzzing around like handsome film extras; school groups and tourists, huddled and self-contained. It was January but mild, and Christmas lights still clung to buildings. The city air mingled with diesel fumes and garlic; I breathed in those smells, while negotiating my way around the cars abandoned on broken footpaths. It was odd to be on my own – I never spent much time alone – but I was enjoying the peace of it and the freedom. It felt like I had the city to myself as I trailed some of the lonelier streets.

At the Trevi Fountain I tossed a two-euro coin into the water – it was a different currency when I did the same thing on my honeymoon, full of mad hope. Eddie spent most of the holiday drinking beer in cafés, while I sipped lemonade and watched him warily. I turned from the Trevi and saw a young man approach one of the gladiator tour guides with his camera; the gladiator shook his head and gestured for him to go away. The man turned and shrugged at his wife.

'Excuse me,' I said, 'I'll take your picture if you like.' I made photo-taking movements with my hands, in case they didn't understand.

'Oh, thank you so much,' the wife said, in an American accent, settling her baby onto her hip.

I snapped and snapped while the three of them cuddled in front of the rock-faced fountain. The baby was happy and huge-eyed, like Martha had been. Eddie used to call Martha 'Smiley Biscuit Face' when she was very small. Things had been good at times – when he wanted them to be. He never saw

Martha after I left him. She pretended that was all right, but I knew it hurt that he couldn't drag himself away from Grogan's Bar to spend even an hour with her.

'Your baby is gorgeous,' I said to the couple.

'So we are told.' The husband laughed.

'The Italian people love her,' the wife said. 'We get "bella, bella" all day. They pinch her cheeks.'

'I have a daughter; she's seventeen now,' I said. 'Little girls are wonderful. "Bella" is right.'

The couple smiled, thanked me again and walked away, one hand each on their baby's buggy. I threw another coin in the fountain to wish them a long, happy marriage; and one for Martha to keep her safe while I was away. Then I headed back to the hotel to sleep.

In the morning, the louvered window-shutters threw a ladder of light across my bed. I had breakfast at the Trattoria Coriolano; the forecast had promised rain so I dressed for it, but the day was bright. The moustachioed waiter greeted me with 'Ciao Bella' and I smiled. He brought the latté and Viennese shortbread I ordered. I lingered over them, planning my visit to all the places Eddie and I had been, to take them back for myself, own them anew. That meant choosing between Saint Peter's, the Colosseum and the Mouth of Truth. I settled on the Colosseum because I liked the sense of space all around it. I took a Metro and sat beside a regal old woman who reeked of perfume and dignity.

The sun shone over the Colosseum and I stood opposite, marvelling at the very fact of it. I wandered down the road and crossed when I could; the traffic was heavy. I was at a souvenir stall, paying for a Romulus and Remus keyring for Martha, when a fight broke out between a group of teenage boys; a girl stood to one side, crying into her scarf. I turned to look, along with the stallholder and everyone else. Two boys tossed and tumbled, pulling at each other's hair and shoulders, throwing kicks where they could. The boys grunted and shouted at each other in Italian and their friends hustled around them, alternately egging them on and trying to rip them apart. One of the boys had blood streeling from his nose and the sight of it set the girl with the scarf wailing.

'Ricardo!' she shouted. 'Ricardo!'

'Can't you do something?' I said to the stallholder; he shrugged and went back to serving his other customers.

I had a rolled-up umbrella in my hand. I moved towards the scuffling boys, thinking I could surprise one of them into stopping if I hit him with it. They were moving fast, spinning head-to-head while gripping each other's shoulders. I could smell sweat and deodorant oozing from them. I whacked the nearest boy on the back of the neck with the umbrella and he flung his head up; that made him topple backwards and I watched as he dragged the other boy, crablike, away with him. As they scurried, they knocked the girl with the scarf off the path and she stumbled in front of an oncoming car. The driver jammed on the brakes, but he hit the girl and her body was thrown upwards, like a rag being caught on the wind. There was a loud thwack as she hit the tarmac and people surged forward to see better. Someone screamed.

I backed away, my breath clogging up my neck. 'Oh God,' I said, 'oh my God.'

The crowd parted and I saw the driver of the car kneeling over the girl. One of the teenage boys was cradling her head and crying. Blood seeped onto his denim jacket. The man from the souvenir stall put his hand on my arm and stared at me.

'Signora,' he said. I shook him off, turned, and ran. 'Signora!' he shouted.

I made my way up the Via de Fori Imperiali to the Metro station. I kept looking behind me, then along the station platform when I reached it, but no one followed or tried to talk to me. I trembled all over and willed the train to arrive.

'Please, come quickly,' I said, 'please, please.'

I looked at the umbrella still in my hand, like something alien; as I stepped onto the Metro, I let it drop down between the train and the platform, onto the tracks.

Back at the hotel, I sat on my bed feeling as if I had been turned inside out. My breastbone ached and my lips were tight. I fumbled in my bag for my mobile phone and rang Martha.

'It's me,' I said.

'Mam, I'm at school; you'll get me into trouble.'

'Sorry,' I said, gulping down tears, 'sorry. Martha…'

'Are you OK? How's Rome?'

'It's lovely, yes, good. And I'm fine, love, fine. I miss you, that's all. I miss you.' I swiped at my streaming eyes with a tissue.

'Mam, are you crying? You're such a sap, you've only been gone a day. I have to go, the bell is ringing.'

'Martha, I love you. Be careful crossing the road, sweetheart. Please, do that for me. Be careful.'

'What?'

'I saw a crash today, that's all. It spooked me.'

'Oh. OK, sure, I'll take care.' I could imagine her rolling her eyes. 'Look, I'll talk to you later, Mam. Remember, bring me back something nice. Bye.'

I clutched the mobile to my chest and lay down on the bed; sobs shuddered through me. When I woke, it was dark.

The moon hung low over the basilica; its borrowed light made the golden Jesus dazzle. I tilted my head back and looked from Jesus to the moon, from the moon to Jesus.

'Help me,' I said, not sure to whom I was sending the prayer.

A man walked up and stood nearby; he peed lavishly against the wall of the basilica then looked over at me and laughed. I pushed at the church door and dipped inside. It was warm in there; the yellow paintwork and white pillars shone under dim lights. I made my way to a votive stand and knelt on the prie-dieu. A huge flaming heart set into the ceiling seemed to pulse above my head. I pushed money into the slot and lit a candle for the girl who got knocked down; I lit one for Martha and one for myself. I put my hand over my own heart and begged forgiveness for leaving the accident at the Colosseum.

'Please let the girl be all right,' I said. 'I'm sorry for running away.'

I muttered a Hail Mary – the only prayer I could remember from a childhood filthy with prayer. I stood up to leave, then stopped and shoved one more coin into the stand. I lit a candle for Eddie and wished for good things for him: for sobriety and sense and love; and for anything else he might want.

Back out on the Via Marsala, it had begun to rain. I looked for the moon. It had moved further up into the sky and it hovered there, clean and fresh, urging the world on to new and better things.

Queen of Tattoo

Lydia is big; a ripe tomato of a woman. Men dream about holding her body close; women want to slap her face. But Lydia sits, pleased as pike, on the porch of her house on Cherry Street, sipping lemonade. She rocks there, looking like an outsized ham hock that has a layer of tattoos where the rind should be.

Mr Petruzelli sits by Lydia; he likes to talk up a raving storm and, lucky for him, Lydia likes to listen. Mr Petruzelli calls Lydia his love apple; she calls him Mr Pee. He helps her out with this and that; he is a man who is good with his hands. Lydia says he can fix broken things and open locks just by looking at them. Some say Mr Petruzelli lives right there in the house on Cherry Street with Lydia.

Lydia throws her hands up when she tells a story and lights two cigarettes at a time. She laughs like a man, long and low, from a place deep in her gut. Lydia is a work of art and an artist all in one skin. Tattooed on her back she has the Battle of Waterloo, beside that the wreck of the Hesperus, and above it waves the Stars and Stripes. Lydia sports the city of Paris, the rush of Niagara Falls and Alcatraz – her body is both geography and history.

Lydia doesn't just wear ink, she gives it too. She has a parlour in the front room of her house; there she is the queen of tattoo. Sailors and sirens wander into Lydia and she colours them up and fills them in until they cannot take any more. But one thing Lydia does not do is tattoo the people she loves.

Lydia has a son but no one talks about him. That boy was precious and wrong. The things he did. But this day – the day we are looking at here – Lydia's son shows up. Clyde strolls along Cherry Street wondering about the lid of cloud that is coming down over the rooftops; it has not yet blotted out the sun but he can see that it soon will. He scuffles his feet through the dust, delaying his arrival at his mother's door. Clyde kicks ball with a few kids, then plucks a pink rose from behind a fence and shoves it into his buttonhole. He looks at the crawl space under Lydia's house and remembers the clammy weight of its blackness around his body when he was a young boy. When he sidles up by the porch, he sees Mr Pee bent low in front of his mother; Lydia's neck is thrown back and her fingers dangle over the arms of her chair. Mr Pee's head jiggles and this makes Clyde stop and stare; he moves closer and sees that the man is painting his mother's toenails.

'Hey Mama,' Clyde says, hitching his vest with his thumbs. He turtles his neck up and down inside his collar, and his hat bobs.

Lydia lifts her sunglasses and looks at him for a long moment. 'Clyde,' she says. You would think she had seen him yesterday the way she sits, eyeballing that boy, but she hasn't been in his company for twenty-six months. 'Come and give your mama a hug.' Mr Pee gets up and lets Clyde go to Lydia. He slips his arms around his mother's neck and they hold each other, then Lydia whacks her son on the side of his head. 'That's for not writing me.'

'I know,' Clyde says, and he doesn't allow his hand to rise and comfort his ear.

'Mr Pee, fetch my boy a lemonade. He looks hot and itchy.'

'Yes I will,' Mr Petruzelli says, glancing at Lydia's son like he might be carrying a catching disease. He goes through the screen door and returns quickly, with a jug and a glass on a tray. Mr Pee pours for Clyde then sits by Lydia.

Clyde stretches his dusty legs out on the porch and slurps at the lemonade; he looks around, a hawk beaking the air for prey. The heavy clouds skim low over Cherry Street and then, pop, the sun disappears and it grows dark. A green lizard hurries along the porch rail, looking for a place to rest.

'Mama, I need something from you.'

'Don't I know it, son.'

Clyde pokes the brim of his hat with one finger. 'Some fellas from the penitentiary don't like me much and they're coming after me.'

'And you're thinking you can hide out here.'

'No, Mama, that's not it at all. What I want is for you to help me to change myself, so those fellas don't realise they are looking at Clyde Speer no more.'

'Strikes me you should change your name first,' Mr Petruzelli says. 'And your swagger.'

'Listen to Mr Pee, Clyde.'

'Will you do it, Mama?'

'What am I gonna do, son? Tattoo your face?'

'Just do something. Anything to make me different to who I am.'

Lydia grunts. 'Son, you know I don't ink the people I love. Look at Mr Pee here – he's as plain as a glass of water.'

Mr Petruzelli winks at Lydia and rolls up his shirt-sleeves to show Clyde his arms; he hitches his trouser legs and displays his ruined – but bare – shins.

'I'm in trouble, Mama. Deep trouble. I was hoping you would see that.'

'I see it all right, Clyde. But it seems to me you got yourself in it. Just like last time. So maybe you should get yourself out of it too.'

Lydia lifts her glass to her lips and winces when a slice of lemon catches on her tongue. The air grows leaden with the smell of hot earth and sulphur. Hailstones start to fall, pinging first one at a time, then dropping from the sky in one big rush, like an avalanche of gum balls.

'Whoo-eeee, if that don't beat all.' Lydia points at the hail and she and Mr Pee laugh and laugh.

Clyde runs into the roadway, the ice-balls thrashing at his shoulders; he swoops his hat from his head, holds it out and lets it fill with hailstones. He walks back up the porch steps, kneels down and places the hat in Lydia's lap.

'They look like a hundred tiny moons,' she says, picking a stone from the hat and holding it up for Mr Pee.

Clyde takes his mother's hand and holds it to his face. 'Can you help me, Mama? I need your help real bad.'

Lydia tips the hailstones over the porch floorboards and pushes her son's hat back onto his head. 'Let me see what I can do,' she says.

'I thank you, Mama.'

Lydia puts Clyde lying out like a corpse. 'Safe in the arms of Jesus,' she says, her blessing for each person she inks. She makes the sign of the cross on herself, tipping her fingers from forehead to breast, from shoulder to shoulder. Mr Pee stands to her right and he hands Lydia the sponge and water. Lydia washes Clyde down like he is a baby once more; she takes a towel and dries off her son.

'All ready, my little love apple?' Mr Petruzelli asks.

Lydia nods and Mr Pee hands her the machine; she flicks the switch and its mosquito buzz fills her ears. She lets the sound run through her like whiskey, warming her; she rolls her wrist, waggles her head and grimaces.

'Clyde,' she says, 'the first thing we need to give you is a heart.'

Clyde raped a girl. He was arrested and charged only with assault. The girl still lives in town but she stays inside all the time. Her name is Rosary and they say her father was a priest, but nobody knows if that's true. Rosary lives on Fire Street and she has two restless children. Her husband was shot dead long before Clyde ever clapped eyes on Rosary and wanted that girl for his own.

'Rosary O'Hara is a prisoner in her own home,' Lydia says, wiping blood and ink from Clyde's chest. She has given him a dripping heart with two daggers wedged through the meat of it.

Clyde shrugs. 'Means nothing to me.'

'It means nothing to you? After what you put her through?' Lydia turns off the machine and stares at her son. 'I went over there after you were gone, but Rosary couldn't even look at me, let alone open her mouth to speak.'

Mr Petruzelli frowns at Clyde. 'Your mama left Miss O'Hara a basket of goods, right there at her front door.'

Lydia nods. 'That fine girl, cooped up like a chicken with her two fine boys.'

'A damn shame,' Mr Petruzelli says, 'a crying, honest-to-goodness shame.'

'Amen,' says Lydia. She lifts her gaze to the window and sees the lizard still on the porch rail, nuzzling at the air with his tongue. She looks down at Clyde. How did my boy get this way? 'Flip over, son.'

Clyde turns onto his stomach with a grunt. Lydia surveys the canvas of his back, the pure, pink stretch of it. She washes him down, towels his skin and switches on the machine. Her mind fills with serpents. She thinks of her Bible, of the prince who was like a wolf devouring prey 'to shed blood, and to destroy souls, to get dishonest gain.' The image of the wolf rises up before her eyes, bigger than the snake she was first tempted by, and she begins to tattoo it beneath her son's shoulder blades.

Lydia gets lost in the rhythm of her work. Mr Petruzelli stays by her to sponge Clyde's red, swelling flesh of blood, so Lydia can keep going. She starts with the yellow eyes and builds the face out from there. After a couple of hours the boy begins to whimper but his mother doesn't take any notice. Her own arms, lively with mermaids and anchors, are steady and true as she brings out the picture in her mind onto the skin of her son. The wolf's claws give her particular satisfaction – they bend in horrible points, sharper even, it seems to Lydia, than her tattoo needle.

'Lydia,' Mr Pee says; she doesn't appear to hear him. 'Lydia, my love.' He places his hand gently into the small of her back. 'Why don't you take a rest?'

She looks at him with waxy eyes, the machine still purring in her fist; then she nods and comes back to herself.

'Sit up, Clyde.'

Her son sits, then lifts himself from the table in a daze and walks out onto the porch.

Lydia lies where Clyde lay, her hands across her stomach; Mr Petruzelli rubs her feet and hums a high, pointless tune. He lights a cigarette for her and she smokes it long and slow, tipping the ash into the palm of Mr Pee's willing hand.

'Take the military position,' Lydia says, gripping Clyde's arm between her fingers. He sits on the table and pulls his elbows close to his sides. She wipes his skin, says 'Safe in the arms of Jesus', and blesses herself quickly.

Lydia inks a curved line from his wrist to his armpit. This will be the serpent. She conjures the snake in her mind's eye and starts to put in the scales; this is miniscule, intricate work. She holds her breath and completes one tiny patch at a time.

Clyde sighs and shifts.

'Keep still.'

'I'm just about sore all over. You're hurting me, Mama.'

'Not half as much as you hurt that girl, Clyde.'

He pouts his lower lip. 'It wasn't like they say. Rosary and me have an understanding.'

For the second time Lydia hits her son on the side of the head. 'Are you done with crazy talk?'

Clyde cradles his ear with his fist. 'I love Rosary O'Hara and she loves me. And I can prove it.'

'Go on then.'

Lydia stands back and Clyde slides from the table and picks up his jacket. From the inside pocket he takes a bundle of letters, tied up with string. He hands them to Lydia; she keeps one eye on her son while she slips a letter from its envelope.

'I love you, Clyde,' she reads, 'you are my only true love and I wait for you night and day. You done me no wrong.' Lydia slips out a second page and holds it up. 'Come back to me, Clyde. You are so fine to me. Love Rosarie.'

Lydia knows the child's way Clyde uses language; she recognises the peculiar slant of his vowels, the back and forth mess of all his words. She also knows how Rosary spells her name.

She points a finger at him. 'Keep away from Rosary O'Hara. I mean it, son.'

Clyde rolls from his bed and pulls on his boots; he listens to a dog barking an angry conversation with the night. He squints out the window to where the moon is slung low over the rooftops.

'Good evening, Miss Moon,' he says.

Clyde smokes one of Lydia's cigarettes on the porch, before trotting the length of Cherry Street and turning right. Rosary's house sits at the bottom of Fire Street, a little apart from the other houses, like an afterthought. Its faded yellow boards seem to glow under the moon's light and this makes Clyde stop, put his hands on his hips, and smile.

'I'm back, baby girl,' he whispers into the still air.

It takes Clyde a while to find a way in; unlike last time, the windows and doors are battened tight. He shuffles through the undergrowth around the house, tripping on grass tufts and abandoned toys. Scrabbling around the walls of Rosary's house, he finds the basement trap door under a tangle of weed. He unbolts it, lifts the door and makes his way down one stairs and up another until he is standing in the kitchen. It smells sweet there, like sugared almonds, and Clyde breathes in as if he were breathing on Rosary's skin.

Shadows move outside the walls and within them. Clyde knows this house and he starts to feel so at ease that he whistles a little tune to himself right there in the kitchen. He turns on the light and takes down the hand mirror that Rosary keeps over the sink. Examining his face, he slicks his eyebrows with a wet forefinger and pushes spit through gnashed teeth.

'Mmm,' Clyde says, approving himself.

The kitchen door opens and Clyde swings around, his jaw loose with anticipation. Before her name can form on his lips, he sees that Rosary is holding a gun by her side. Her whole body shakes like a person having a fit; even Rosary's head wobbles and her face looks uncertain but mean. Clyde puts up his hands and backs away, letting the mirror clatter to the floor where it smashes into splinters of bad luck.

'Rosary,' he says, 'hold on girl.'

The bang of the back door flinging open makes Clyde jump like a jackrabbit; he turns to see Mr Petruzelli standing there; he laughs with relief. He lifts one hand to Mr Pee as if he might take his fingers and kiss the knuckles. Rosary stalks across the kitchen towards Clyde, her bare feet making no sound.

'Rooty tooty aim and shooty,' she says, lifting the gun and pulling the trigger.

Clyde falls, a cowboy swoon that looks rehearsed, so slow does he go, knees buckling, back arching, arms flailing. Lydia appears at Rosary's door just as Clyde hits the floor, blood spurting comically from his chest. And then there is silence, until a low moan from Lydia and the sound of her knees hitting the floorboards jolts through it. She cradles her son in her arms and blesses him, tipping her fingers from forehead to breast, from shoulder to shoulder.

'His eyes can't see anymore,' Mr Petruzelli says.

'Safe in the arms of Jesus,' Lydia says, over and over, 'safe in the arms of Jesus.'

Mr Pee kneels behind Lydia and holds her, placing his arms over her arms which are lively with mermaids and anchors, and hearts dropping blood.